French Kiss

Beth Roberts

Mandarin

A Mandarin Paperback
FRENCH KISS
First published in Great Britain 1995
by Mandarin Paperbacks
an imprint of Reed International Books Ltd
Michelin House, 81 Fulham Road, London sw3 6rb
and Auckland, Melbourne, Singapore and Toronto

Based on an original screenplay by Adam Brooks of the
Polygram Filmed Entertainment picture *French Kiss*

All characters and events in French Kiss
*are fictitious, and no resemblance to actual
persons, living or dead, is intentional*

A CIP catalogue record for this title
is available from the British Library
ISBN 0 7493 2235 7

Printed and bound in Great Britain
by Cox & Wyman Ltd, Reading, Berks.

1

CHARLIE LIKED TO SAY THAT IT WAS KATE'S occasional need for adventure that brought her to Canada, but that it was her greater need to settle down that kept her there. Charlie also liked to think that it was exactly this combination and proportion of characteristics that made Kate the perfect girl for him. As he drove himself through the rigours of medical school he would often stop to daydream about Doctor Charlie and Kate Lytton of Toronto, out to get a big piece of the world – steadily, and together. He didn't have a precise vision of where or how they were going to end up; Charlie was still at the stage where he was content with vague feelings of progress and growing sensations of pleasure, pride and comfort.

Kate, on the other hand, could practically draw a map from the here and now to her distant future, including address changes and job promotions.

Kate Taylor had moved to Canada from her childhood home in Akron, Ohio. Devoted to her adopted country, she loved all the clichés and other aspects of Canadian life that everyone joked about. She loved how eager people were to be recognised by the world, how clean the streets were and how friendly everyone was. She even loved the way people lined up at bus-stops. But what she loved most was something that the Canadians could not see themselves: Canada was a brilliant mixture of North American novelty and deeply British ceremony and politeness. In short, a British colony lost in the Americas. The perfect place to start a new life and family. And falling in love with Charlie was like falling in love with Canada itself.

She had met him the first time she came to Toronto – for a teacher's conference on the future of public education. Her trip turned out to be one marvel after another, culminating at a fabulous party in the expensive but tasteful Rosedale home of a fellow teacher's parents. They also happened to be the parents of Charlie's best friend, and Kate and Charlie's love affair was born on the central stairway, between a living-room full of teachers dancing and a dining-room full of doctors drinking themselves into the courage to dance.

So Kate found a job, got a work visa and moved to Toronto permanently. Charlie, graduating, searched carefully and took a position in a prestigious University Avenue medical practice. In celebration of his success and long-awaited independence, he insisted that Kate move in with him right away. They chose a modern but comfortable town house near Bloor Street, painted it beige and taupe and white, and got very comfortable in a very short time.

They had been living together for several months when Kate let Charlie in on her small but significant secret. For Kate, all travel was train travel. If no train could reach their destination, a car or bus would have to do.

'So all that stuff about the romance of the railroad and the architectural beauty of Union Station was . . . ?'

3

'I don't know why I like trains, Charlie, I'm just happy that I do, or I wouldn't be able to go anywhere.'

'So when is the last time you flew in a plane?' Charlie asked.

'The first and the last time was in tenth grade. Jimmy Gladstone's father flew the whole class to Sioux Island in this tiny, flimsy twin-engine propellor plane for a camping trip. I refused to get back in the plane to get home. They had to pretend I was having an appendicitis attack to get a water ambulance in to take me off the island.'

'You haven't been on a plane for ten years?' Charlie was incredulous.

'Eight years, and don't worry, it won't go on for ever. I'm working on it. Trust me.' Kate made sure she caught his eye, and smiled at him confidently. 'By the time we go on our honeymoon, I'll be ready to climb the rolling staircase up to an airplane.'

'They don't use those rolling staircases any more.'

Charlie was surprised to find this out about the woman he planned to marry. He wondered how he could know so much about someone and not have a clue about something as neurotic as this.

He also wondered, half humorously, how his family would take the news. They were as crazy about Kate as he was, maybe even more so. So far, she had been the paragon of girlfriend-hood, but they were very serious about their vacations in far-away and hard-to-get-to places.

It would be Charlie, though, who would provide the first big test of Kate's newly acquired courage.

2

'OKAY,' KATE DECLARED, OVERCOMING HER FEAR
of airplanes was going to be her highest priority.
First she researched the options – analysis, hyp-
nosis, meditation, medication and therapy groups.
Finally she settled upon the U CAN FLY programme
that, although new and experimental, was recom-
mended by the major airlines. After the first month,
she wondered why all self-help programmes felt so
much like kindergarten classes. She couldn't get rid
of the feeling that she ought to be exempt from
this silliness, that her problem wasn't quite as usual or as facile as the others in the group. But she

was determined to go the whole way through. She promised herself that she was going to succeed and that she'd try the flight simulator, which would carry her through a trial jet take-off and landing before she entertained the idea of giving up. She reminded herself that her money would be fully refunded if the programme failed.

On the day of her big test in the simulator, Kate ceremoniously dressed herself as if she were taking a trip. Although she had a full day of teaching before her appointment, she thought of nothing but the roar of engines, the smell of ozone and the sensation of G-forces pressing her body against rough, institutional chair upholstery. It was scheduled for 5.00 that afternoon. She paced herself all day long. She behaved very deliberately. It was as if courage were measured in calories and she was being rationed.

Kate clutched the armrests of the airplane and tried to pinch the seat cushion with the back of her knees. The more she tried to relax, the tighter her grip became. She tried to concentrate on the smooth and monotonous voice that was speaking over the PA system.

'Welcome to Air Canada's non-stop service

from Toronto to Paris. Our flying time today is estimated to be seven hours and twenty minutes. Please check that your seat belt is fastened and that your chair back is in the upright position. We'll be taking off shortly. We hope you have a pleasant flight . . .'

As she heard the engines roar to life, Kate's fingers tightened and her eyes squeezed shut. It was as though she were trying to lock everything up very tightly, so that the old images of disaster couldn't penetrate her new armour.

As she pulled further into herself for strength she heard her name.

'Kate.'

'Yes,' she replied haltingly. It was the voice from the PA – her instructor Patricia's voice. It reminded her of Hal, the talking computer in the movie *2001*.

'Are you prepared to have a pleasant flight?' When Kate shook her head, Patricia's smooth voice continued, 'Tell me Kate, what are you thinking about?'

As if in a trance, Kate replied, 'Twisted steel. Balls of fire. And a little naked baby screaming for its mama.'

'What's wrong, Kate? What happened to your image of calm and serenity? What happened to your beautiful countryside setting? Now let's go back. Let's try to picture it now.'

Kate felt like a little white mouse in a laboratory experiment. She shifted uncomfortably in her chair as Patricia continued.

'Now don't forget you take-off mantra. Chant the words slowly and softy in your head. What is your mantra, Kate?'

Kate took a big breath to help release the tension. But when she opened her mouth, all that came out was, 'We're going down we're going down we're going down in a blaze of fire and melting steel.'

'Kate. Let's get back on track. Now, your mantra.'

Patricia carefully peeked out from her place behind the curtain. Even though Kate's eyes were shut, Patricia could see her eyeballs rolling in disgust. Yet Kate went on. 'I love Paris in the springtime. I love Paris in the fall . . . fall . . . fall . . .' Her eyes snapped open. 'I really think you gave me the wrong mantra.'

'Everyone thinks they got the wrong mantra, Kate.' Patricia was getting irritated, but hoping that her snarkiness would quiet Kate down. She continued to breathe slowly and deeply and regularly, over the loudspeaker, in an effort to influence Kate, who was looking increasingly agitated.

'No. You see I don't love Paris, I hate the French and I don't want to go on this trip.'

Patricia had dealt with tougher cases. She was sure she could salvage the run and give Kate the feeling of a successful take-off, if she could just show her how far they'd already come. She curled her fingertips around her controls and gently pushed a tiny button hidden from view. As soon as she did, the engines roared louder and electronic beeps sounded in warning of an imminent ascent. The pilot's voice announced, 'Flight attendants prepare for take-off.'

Kate quietly heaved an 'Oh, God . . .'

'Kate, you can do this.' The voice was still patronising and a little too insistent.

'I can't. I don't belong in an airplane. Even this one.' Kate sat up in a state of contained panic. She caught a glimpse of the runway rushing beneath her. She reached down and unbuckled her seatbelt with one smooth swipe across her lap. She was up and out into the aisle with one broad sideways step. She rushed toward the huge pneumatic exit door. As she frantically pulled the long lever upwards, she thought she could hear Patricia speaking to her.

'No,' Kate cried, 'Let me out. I don't want to die, we're going to die in here.' The adrenalin rush that she got from screaming helped her to yank the lever all the way up. She threw her shoulder into the curved plastic surface and swung the huge door open, hurling herself out.

The thud of her landing on the concrete floor beneath the simulator startled her. After a dazed moment, Kate raised her head in relief, with a triumphant grin directed at Patricia and the lab technicians who were now hulking over her. She let her eyes fall on the filmed backdrop of clouds as she lifted herself up off the floor and turned to leave the studio.

She felt no guilt about her actions. The programme had failed her. She sat down in the director's office and stared at her until she got off the phone. 'I think it's time for my refund. I'm sure this works for everyone else. But I'll just take the cheque,' she said politely, rubbing her sore shoulder as she waited for the cheque to be written. She reached for it slowly and folded it neatly before she flashed a triumphant smile and left the building.

It was several nights later, as he was finishing his packing and preparing to leave for the airport, that Charlie made his final pitch to get Kate to reconsider. This was his dream trip. Ten days in Paris, France. Capital of food, wine, romance and fun.

'Come on, Kate,' he pleaded. 'I'll give you ten milligrams of valium, a shot of vodka on ice and the next thing you know we'll be there. How can you refuse a trip to Paris? You're a history teacher for God's sake.'

Kate shook her head. 'Listen, Charlie. From a history teacher's point of view, the French have a lot of ugly skeletons in the closet. Name a century and I'll go down the list. And besides, they have a thing about dairy products that I just can't live with. I'd have to make substitutions several times a meal . . .'

Before she could finish her rehearsed speech, they heard Charlie's parents calling from the bottom of the stairs. Charlie cringed a little. 'Have you noticed how since we became engaged they never knock?' He made one last offensive. 'I've got to admit I was looking forward to being alone with you. A week in Paris by ourselves, in love. Sidewalk cafés, midnight strolls along the Seine, the Eiffel Tower . . .'

Kate drifted off for a minute. 'Yes, I'd like to see the Eiffel Tower . . .' But she caught herself as she saw she was giving Charlie false hope. 'But too bad that I'm not allowed to leave the country until after my immigration interview. They'd find out, Charlie. They would. It's like the one time in my whole life that I smoked pot. One pathetic little time. I didn't want to do it in the first place. I had a horrible experience. And then to top it off Ronnie Templeton's little brother called the police on us. We were all arrested! The only time I ever did *anything* illegal.'

Before Charlie could respond, his sister Lilly poked her head into the room. 'Do you guys want to eat up here?' she asked. Fifteen years old, Lilly had the right mixture of interest in life and adolescent brazenness toward adults. She had become very close to Kate, won over by the idea of having another woman in the family.

Charlie raised an eyebrow. 'No thank you, Lilly. We'll be down in a minute. We're talking right now.'

Lilly walked in with her plate of pizza and got comfortable on the bed. 'Oh yeah? What about?'

Their discussion was clearly over. Annoyed with this constant and total invasion by his family, Charlie sighed with exasperation. He was a grown man, for heaven's sake. This was his third trip to Europe. His entire family did not need to come and see him off. But for some reason Kate liked it. She was still enthralled with his family. It was what she'd always wanted.

He watched as Kate and Lilly left the room

and headed downstairs, laughing and whispering. They were remarkably relaxed and intimate with each other. He couldn't figure out if he hated it, resented it, or was just scared that Kate would come to adopt the attitudes his family had about him. He hated couples who disappeared into their families like more kids into the mix. It was un-romantic and it was depressing.

He finished packing, trying to anticipate his trip to Paris. He was excited but wished he wasn't going alone.

As soon as Kate got downstairs, she met Char-lie's mother in the hallway. Rose Lytton was slender, noble and silver-haired. She had incred-ible powers of persuasion that she put to use a great deal, but always with grace and elegance. She was waiting for the right moment to speak so that her husband Herb, who was sitting in the living-room engrossed in a hockey game on the TV, would hear her. During a pause in the game she spoke affectionately and apologetically. 'Kate darling, it looks like both pizzas have arrived with cheese on them. We ordered one with tofu cheese, but I guess Herb didn't check.' She tossed her head toward her husband and spoke firmly. 'You should go back, dear, and get the right one.'

Herb looked guiltily in their direction and was

about to speak when Kate interjected, 'Don't worry. I'll pick it off . . . Really.' Herb brightened considerably, motioned to his wife that it was all settled and returned his attention to the game. Kate smiled reassuringly at Rose.

Somewhat reluctantly, Charlie came downstairs and stopped to listen to the hockey game for a moment. As he stood behind the sofa watching the players scurrying over the ice and listening to the din of the crowd on TV he could hear the conversation between his mother, sister and Kate in the kitchen. It was clear that everyone still thought that Kate was going to Paris with him. When Lilly began to ask Kate for a short list of souvenirs from France, he decided that he'd heard enough. 'Kate's not going,' he called out. 'She has decided to stay here.'

No one missed a beat. 'Is it the immigration thing?' asked Lilly.

'Well, her immigration appointment is next month. I can understand her caution,' Rose said, completely supportive of her future daughter-in-law.

'It's not the immigration thing. It's the flying thing,' Charlie said flatly. Until now there had been an unspoken pact in the family. Everyone knew about the flying thing but they never mentioned the problem. They were all so confident that she'd get over it. Now they were behaving like she was being brilliantly sensible; as though she really should let the remote possibility of being caught by the immigration police be an excuse for passing up a free trip to Paris. Charlie was incredulous. Kate could do no wrong.

Charlie tried to get everyone's attention off the issue. 'Kate, we should get going in case there's a lot of traffic on the way to the airport.'

In fact, there was plenty of time. But one by one, everyone started to prepare to leave, sensing Charlie's uneasiness with the open airing of his life's details. As Charlie watched them clear up, he felt relieved.

As he pulled on his trench coat, his dad lit up with an announcement. 'Oh, by the way, I've just found out that the Merediths are putting their house on the market. If you're still interested maybe I could talk to them.' Charlie froze. He wasn't sure why, but the news made him feel very anxious.

'Charlie!' Kate called to him excitedly from the kitchen, where she'd gone with the last pile of paper plates and napkins. 'Charlie, did you hear that news?' If Paris was Charlie's dream come true, the Merediths' for sale sign was Kate's.

She swung into high gear, ecstatic, consumed with anticipation. 'Charlie? . . . Charlie?' She waited for a moment and then realised that he was not going to say anything.

3

ONCE THEY WERE IN THE CAR TOGETHER, KATE
convinced Charlie to stop by the Merediths' house
and just look at it for a minute. 'What happens if
someone puts a bid in while you're away and we
have to act fast?' she asked. She was trying to seem
calmer and less excited than she actually was, well
aware of Charlie's ambivalence.

They drove two blocks north and turned
on to a block of modest but elegant brick and
stucco Tudor homes. Charlie parked across the
street from the Merediths', which stood out
for its intricately landscaped yard. The house

emitted a golden light from the chandeliers that hung in the foyer and living-room. Little bits of brass hardware shone, the garbage cans were in perfect order. It all looked terribly grown-up.

Charlie stared at the house for a moment. He saw the Merediths, an elderly couple, moving around the living-room with ease and familiarity. 'Kate. Why are we looking at a house that we can't afford?' Houses in this neighbourhood were dear and rare.

Kate took a deep breath and let it out in a long, loud, tension-relieving blow. 'Charlie, there's something that I want to tell you.' She prepared herself for a significant but short story. 'Ever since I was twenty-one, I've put a little money aside, every week of my adult life. It was all in a savings account which I rolled over into some high-yield term deposits at a very good time. The interest rates reached fourteen per cent.'

'What are you talking about?' Charlie was still watching the Merediths. He couldn't figure out if they were tinkering with each other's buttons or having an argument.

'I've made us a nest egg,' said Kate bluntly.

Charlie barely glanced at her. 'How many

eggs, Kate?' He was perplexed. He realised that he was in for more news.

'Sixty-two thousand eggs.' Then she added, 'American.'

Charlie finally took his eyes off the Merediths and looked at Kate. 'Wow. That's over seventy-five thousand, Canadian. Why didn't you tell me this before?'

'I wanted it to be a surprise.' Kate started to chew on the inside of her cheek as she waited for his response.

But Charlie just nodded his head, almost imperceptibly. Finally he whispered, 'It's a surprise . . . A big surprise.'

Kate couldn't tell how Charlie felt about the news. She was nervous and was having trouble reading him. To tip the scales she added, 'I've thought about it, and with a little help from your parents, we could afford this house right now!'

Charlie let out a short, tense giggle. 'Boy,' he said, 'My whole life is passing before my eyes. And it turns out it's my parents' life, not mine . . .'

Kate moved closer and took Charlie's hands off the steering-wheel. Smiling sweetly, as if to dare him, she moved in closer still, fitting herself into the warm curve of his arm and chest. She raised her head to kiss him. They relaxed for a second and kissed a kiss that made them remember how much they were in love.

As Kate watched Charlie's plane take off that night, she imagined them gliding right into the next stage of their life together. Fast and steady, like the plane. She went home that night with a feeling of security and confidence. She longed for the ten days to be over so that they could return to the momentum they were building. She loved the feeling of movement in her life.

The following night, Kate sat curled up on her sofa watching the news. She was the kind of person who hated the news but was transfixed by it because she hated not knowing everything that was going on as soon as it hit the air waves. As the clock flipped from 6.59 to 7.00, the NBC logo flashed onto the screen and the telephone rang. Right on time. Kate smiled contentedly, happy to be saved from the broadcast. 'Hello, there.' She aimed the TV remote control at the screen and pressed the mute button.

'*Bon soir, chérie.*' Charlie spoke confidently and giddily.

'Ooh, good accent. How's it going?' Kate had to wait a second because of the connection. As she listened to the phone she continued to watch the screen.

'Just one seminar after another. But this city, God, it's so beautiful. It casts a spell over you – '

'How was dinner?' she broke in.

'Great. They used this sauce, it had a taste that I've never experienced. Just *incroyable*.'

'Well Charlie, the sauces have to be *incroyable* to cover up the taste of the horsemeat. I saw this really *incroyable* story on *60 Minutes* about it.'

Charlie listened to her comments with a combination of tenderness and distance. He was amazed at how far away from Kate and her neuroses he felt after just twenty-four hours. Finally he replied, 'Hon, if you keep watching all those shows you watch, you won't be able to leave the house.'

In Charlie's absence, Kate continued right on with her plans to put a bid on the house and with their plans for the wedding. She tried to get as much information to and from Charlie as she could during their brief evening chats, but he was hard to pin down, always in a rush. She sensed that although he was clearly happy and having fun, something was odd, and resolved to take her time and try to get him to talk to her, really talk to her, when they spoke again. She was standing in her kitchen unloading groceries when the phone rang. She grabbed the receiver immediately. 'Hi.'

'*Ça va? C'est moi* . . .' Charlie sounded very far away.

'Hi you. Guess what? I talked to the Merediths about their house. They don't have a broker yet. We could save on the commission. What do you think?'

'Sorry honey, but I think this will have to wait. I've got an eight o'clock suture demonstration in the morning and I've got to get some sleep tonight. It feels like it's been weeks.' Charlie trailed off.

Kate blanched. She wasn't sure if he meant that it felt like weeks since he'd slept or since he'd seen her. She spoke haltingly. 'We'll talk about it tomorrow? Because I don't want to blow this. You know what I mean, Charlie?' As she waited for his answer her hand slipped into a drawer and pulled out a huge chocolate bar. She absent-mindedly peeled off the wrapper and began to eat it like a piece of bread.

'We'll try, honey. Honey? I love you. Goodnight.' Charlie was quietly gone.

Kate wasn't altogether surprised to find Charlie in an equally elusive mood again the next day.

Guys never want to buy their first house or get pregnant until after it already happens. She decided to proceed with optimism until she had some undeniable evidence to the contrary. 'Hey!' she said when she heard his voice the next evening.

'Hey,' he replied. 'I can't really talk right now, I just wanted to check in. We're going to this very hip club with some of the guys.'

Kate tried not to take it too personally. 'Sweetie-pie, I really need to talk to you about the house.'

'I know. I promise you. We'll talk tomorrow.' For just one moment he sounded relaxed and tender. Like his old self.

Kate was prepared for their next conversation. She had gone over all of the points she wanted to cover several times by seven o'clock the following evening. But Charlie didn't call on time. By seven-thirty, Kate began to wonder if she'd read the clock wrong. A few minutes later Lilly rang the door bell. Kate had invited her over to have dinner, and she talked to her about the house as they chopped vegetables for a stir-fry.

'I've called the Merediths and told them that we're ready to put in an offer. So when Charlie calls I'm going to have to force a decision. I feel like we've either got to do it or drop it.'

Lilly listened attentively but all the while she

was shaking her head a little bit. At fifteen, she was a little serious about the subject of growing up. 'I'm never going to buy a house or anything else worth anything,' she told Kate.

'Why not?', Kate asked, raising an eyebrow, only half humouring her.

'Well, you think you own something like that, but what I think is that it winds up owning you. It becomes your whole focus: decorating it, keeping it up, painting it, gardening. It's your whole life. Then one night someone forgets to put out their cigarette. Pouf.' She threw up her hands. 'The whole thing burns to the ground. Then where are you?'

Kate looked at her. 'Yeah. But we don't let anyone smoke in our house.' Once she assured herself that she'd got a little smile out of Lilly, Kate glanced nervously at the clock and the telephone.

'Are you guys like this about everything?' Lilly asked, noticing Kate's anxiety.

'No. Charlie's never like this. Never. It's just not like him at all.' Kate listened to herself speak and realised that she was depressing herself – a realisation which was interrupted by the phone. She rushed over to it and put on a brighter voice. 'Hello? Honey?' She strained to listen. It was either a bad connection or Charlie was out at another 'hip' club.

'Kate? Kate . . . ?' Charlie sounded awful.

'It's me, Charlie,' she replied, 'are you all right? Is something wrong?'

Charlie was still sounding strained 'No. Yes. I mean . . . something's happened.'

'What? What happened? What's wrong?' Kate felt a little wild alarm go off in her head. She looked over at Lilly slicing through a red pepper and tried to calm herself. She clutched the telephone cord and the receiver and her gut in one smooth motion.

'Oh, Kate,' he continued, 'I'm so happy and so screwed up . . . I've really screwed up. But it's destiny, I guess, that's what it is. It's gotta be.' He sounded very tired and very drunk.

'What? Charlie. What's destiny? What are you saying?' Kate was trying to sound calm and interested so she could get him to explain what was going on. She felt her stomach tighten.

'It's destiny. Oh Kate, I've met this woman. An apparition. A *goddesse*.'

'A *god-DESSE*?' she mimicked.

'Yeah. It's French for goddess. And so is she. She's French, Kate. Please understand, I've never, ever . . . felt like this before. Like I could do anything. Climb mountains, rule the world, walk right into a crowded men's room and pee with some big guy standing right behind me. Anything.' Charlie started to weep.

'What? What are you saying? . . . What do you mean, Charlie? Are you –' Kate was wildly searching the room for something to rest her eyes upon while she waited for an answer.

'I guess what I'm saying is that I'm not coming back, Kate. I'm in love. Like a sonnet, like a movie, like a . . . like love, Kate. Kate, I'm so sorry.' He hung up the phone. Click. Nothing.

'Charlie . . . ?'

4

ALL THE THERAPY AND TRAINING IN THE WORLD couldn't have done what that phone call did to get Kate on to an airplane. As soon as she had hung up the phone she looked over to Lilly and knew exactly what she had to do. Fly there. Do anything. Face him. Get him back. She knew she could do it. She was not going to let it end like this.

'Welcome to Air Canada flight 716 flying non-stop to Paris.' When Kate heard the familiar, almost nauseating sound of the flight attendant's voice, her response was practically Pavlovian. Her spine stiffened, her eyebrows arched, her stomach ached and her fingers grasped the armrests like claws to a perch. She was kind of glad because she realised that she was expending more energy hating the memory of the fear-flying course than she was on actually being phobic about the coming flight. She wondered if that was what the course intended to do: transfer your dread of flight into a dread of self-help courses . . . She stopped dead as she realised she was only pretending that she wasn't on the verge of hysteria.

'You're in my seat.' Her thoughts were interrupted by a loud and aggressive French voice. She looked up and saw a tall, unshaven, scruffy guy hulking over a businessman sitting two rows up. 'I said, you are in my seat!' the Frenchman continued. He was gruff-looking in his worn leather jacket and thick black jeans, and as he gesticulated he waved nicotine-stained, workmanlike hands.

'I think you've made a mistake,' the businessman responded, firmly but politely.

As Kate watched, her left hand involuntarily moved toward the empty seat next to her. She ran her palm over it, trying to make it look full and unavailable, trying to ignore the flicker of anxiety she felt. The man sitting two seats away, the other side of the empty seat, seemed oblivious to the scene unfolding a few rows in front of them. Odd looking and dressed in an olive-green tweed suit, he was organising his little space for the flight. Pillow here, magazines stacked there, a water bottle within hands' reach and a little sack of gum and candy in the pouch in front of him. He looked like a little anal-retentive astronaut on his way into deep space; the Perfect Passenger.

Kate heard the French guy start to rant again.

'*Quoi?* What? Puh! The only mistake I make was to go to take a piss! Let's go, out, out! I was gone only five minutes.' The Frenchman looked around to the other passengers in an effort to enlist support. None was forthcoming.

A flight attendant authoritatively moved down the aisle toward them. 'Monsieur, please. We can't leave the gate until everyone is sitting down with their seat-belt buckled. Could I please see your boarding pass?' She saw his pass sticking out of his coat pocket and reached for it.

The Frenchman reacted in a predictably rebel-lious fashion and violently swished his coat away from her. As he turned, though, he noticed that she was an extraordinarily beautiful woman, and as only a Frenchman could, he instantly changed gears. He smiled softly, looked her directly in the eye, and offered her his coat pocket gallantly and flirtatiously.

The flight attendant glanced at the boarding pass for a second and then began to run her gaze along the rows to find the seat in question. As she did, Kate touched the empty seat beside her again and chanted a little prayer. Any seat but this. Any seat but this. Please. Please. Please. When she opened her eyes and looked up she saw them all staring directly back at her. Shit.

The Frenchman gathered up his cases and tore down the aisle like a bull. Kate could almost taste the stale tobacco smoke wafting off him. Little wisps of slightly greasy hair clung to his neck and cheek as he cursed his way toward her. By now even the Perfect Passenger in the aisle seat was looking at her, wide-eyed and quizzical. Kate watched as this funny man scrunched up his mouth and nodded as he let the Frenchman pass over his lap. The Frenchman, still indignant and arrogant, looked at Kate and the Perfect Passenger as if he'd been banished to the dunces corner with all the geeks in the class.

Kate decided that the only thing to do was to block him out. She had hoped to sneak the occasional peek at the Perfect Passenger during take-off, while they served the meal, or during turbulence. She was sure that she could get useful pointers from him. Now she would lose her view of him as she tried to avoid the Frenchman. She turned her attention inward and began to mouth her mantra. 'I hate Paris in the springtime, I hate Paris in the fall . . . Why oh why do I hate Paris? Because my love is there . . . courting a slut . . .'

She didn't realise it at first, but she was mumbling. When she opened her eyes, the Frenchman was staring right at her. He didn't say anything. He just kept looking. Like an analyst or something.

'It's my first time,' Kate said politely. 'Flying. So, I'm kind of nervous, you know?' She noticed that his expression didn't change. Slightly annoyed, she held up her index finger and continued, '*First* time? – You speak any English?' He raised an eyebrow but did not respond. Completely turned off by now, Kate added sarcastically, 'Didn't your mother ever teach you about staring? It's impolite.'

He finally spoke. 'What do you think? The plane craches in a ball of fire and everyone is on the ground in a thousand little pieces, dead?'

Kate couldn't believe she had to deal with this arrogant jerk. 'You're French, aren't you?'

Ah! He was impressed. He extended his hand toward her. 'Oui. Luc Teyssier.' When he realised that she wasn't going to take his hand, he shrugged and withdrew it. 'Tell me,' he continued, 'I am curious. How have you got around your whole life? You just stay at home with the door locked?'

Kate pantomimed a let-your-fingers-do-the-walking gesture along the armrest. 'I get around as nature intended,' she told him firmly. 'In a car.' She was interrupted by the flight attendant's voice, speaking over the PA. She spoke in French now, quickly and for a long time, and Kate couldn't make out any of the important words. She looked at Luc. 'What did she say? It sounded serious.'

'Not at all,' he replied with a sleazy smile. 'Something about a small, hair-line crack in the engine case. They fix it *tout de suite*. Right away. Then we're off.'

Kate was instantly nauseous. That's it, she had to get out of here. She undid her seat-belt and began to lift herself up. Then she heard the attendant's voice again, this time in English. 'Ladies and gentlemen, please remember that the use of computers, cellular phones and other electronic devices is forbidden during take-off . . .'

Realising that she'd been had, Kate slumped back into her seat. She was pissed off. 'I don't know what they taught you in France, but rude and interesting are not the same thing.' She was trying to calm down as she spoke. Get herself back into the take-off. But the plane jerked violently as it disengaged from the gate, and she let out an involuntary shriek. She saw Luc's amusement out of the corner of her eye and turned to the window and pulled down the shade. She didn't want to watch what was going on outside. Then she saw the Perfect Passenger studying his laminated emergency instruction card. She pulled hers out of the seat-back in front of her and did the same.

'Folks, we're about third in line for take-off,' came the captain's voice over the PA. 'So just relax, we should be in the air in just a couple of minutes.'

Kate got tenser. She had not been prepared for all the little delays. She clutched the armrest tighter and closed her eyes. She tried to breathe deeply and regularly in an effort to relax, but she sensed that Luc was leaning closer and studying her. She opened her eyes again and turned to him. 'Look,' she said, 'I've almost got an image going here, so could you please stop your – '

'It's incredible,' he remarked.

'What?' she replied. 'What's incredible?'

'That every muscle in your body is . . . tense. Like a fist. Even the lids of your eyes. How do you do that?'

Kate's chance to respond was usurped by the whine of the engines as they revved for take-off. She let out a short, tight gasp.

Luc reached across her confidently and lifted the window blind, then leaned back expectantly. 'Me, I love to fly. *Surtout maintenant.* This moment is great. The plane ready to charge, the engines scream, the pressure mounts, the force of it slams you back and then . . . whoosh . . . *voilà*! You are in the air and everything is vanishing behind you. There is only one other place where I feel this exhilaration.'

'Oh,' said Kate flatly. 'And let me guess where that would be.'

Meanwhile the captain's voice came back to them. 'Flight attendants, prepare for take-off.'

Kate was paralysed. 'I don't think I can do this.'

Luc pulled the laminated card from her grip and calmly smoothed it out before replacing it in the pouch. 'Did you ever think that perhaps it is not the airplane?' he asked in an authoritative voice.

'What's not the airplane?' Kate was irritable.

'Well, maybe it is something else that you are afraid of.' Luc looked so arrogant that Kate felt like smacking him.

'Now what are you talking about?' she snapped. She didn't really want to know.

'Do I have to say?'

Kate smiled sarcastically. 'Am I going to be able to stop you?'

'You are not afraid of the airplane at all. It is obvious to me. I know your type.'

'What *type*?' Kate suddenly stiffened as the engines began to roar again, and the plane started forward. She tried to unbuckle her belt, but Luc put his hand over hers. She slipped hers away more out of revulsion than reassurance.

'You are afraid to live, really live,' he went on. 'You are afraid of life, of love and of good sex.'

She couldn't believe her ears. 'What? You're ridiculous!'

Luc didn't let her reaction stop him. He just continued: 'I can see it in your face, the way you dress, the little shirt buttons done all the way up to your throat.' He gestured at her shirt. 'You are the kind of woman, in bed, you are waiting under the covers, the light is off, and then like a *petite* rabbit . . .' His face performed a revolting impersonation of a rabbit having sex.

'What? *What!*' Kate didn't know whether to laugh or scream. 'How dare you? You don't know anything about me! You don't even know what I do . . . And Charlie never complained, Charlie never . . . There was a short time when . . . but that was ages ago, and I was between jobs and this is *none* of your business! So how can you sit there with that smug expression . . .' She went on, but her words and then her yelling were drowned out by the roar of the plane as it barrelled down the runway and lifted into the air. 'I mean, for you to tell me that I have a problem with my life, with my Charlie, is insane. It's . . . I mean look at you, you're just an arrogant French guy stewed in nicotine!'

Luc ignored her and glanced out of the window. 'What a beautiful view, *non*?' They were airborne. Kate was flying. He grinned and stood up. '*Excusez-moi*, but I must go and do now, as nature intended.' He squeezed past his neighbour, who was still listening to his walkman, and disappeared down the aisle to the WC.

5

LUC WAS GONE A LONG TIME. THE DRINKS AND
dinner service had already begun and Kate didn't
know what to get for him. She asked for the chicken
for herself, because she figured that the Perfect
Passenger would know what was good, and that
was what he'd ordered. She couldn't find a way to
approach it, though, it looked so bloated and
crammed into the small square dish. She was sure it
had been injected with hundreds of chemicals, pre-
servatives and artificial flavours. Her mentor was
eating it, though. He was even enjoying himself.

Luc finally came out of the toilet and moved

past the long line of waiting passengers. As he pushed past the drinks cart he politely asked for a cup of ice. When the flight attendant turned to fill a plastic cup for him, he nimbly grabbed a fistful of little spirits bottles from the top of her cart. The bottles disappeared into the folds of his jacket. He sauntered back to his seat, sat down and began to mix himself a drink. As he poured, he sensed that he was being scrutinised. He looked up, to find Kate staring at him expectantly.

'Excuse me, but, can I ask you something? It's Luke, isn't it?' Kate was polite.

'Luc.' He elongated the '*u*' and added a little '*eh*' sound to the end.

Kate tried it again.

'Non, not Luke, it's *Luuuc*.' He was being patronising now.

Kate's temper returned. Her eyes narrowed as she glared at him. She started to roll a long throaty 'r' sound. 'Rrrrrrrrrrrr . . . That's French, isn't it, *Luuuc-eh*?'

She couldn't get to him. 'You want to ask me some, eh thing, or no?' he responded flatly.

'*Something* is one word, Luc. And no, forget it.' She turned towards the window, fed up.

'*D'accord*. Okay. I forget already.' Luc sat back and acted nonchalant. His eyes roamed around for something new to do. His tray table was covered with a square dinner tray. The food looked disgusting, inedible. But there was nowhere to move it to. He threw his hands up in mock resolve and poured another drink.

By his side, Kate's jaw was tensed. She couldn't let it go. Luc's accusing words were bugging her, gnawing at her: she felt she deserved an explanation. She turned back to him and blurted, 'This is the thing. When we were taking off and you said all that stuff, did you mean it or were you just trying to make me really angry?' She waited for some sign of understanding before continuing, 'I mean, do I look like someone who doesn't know how to have a good time?'

Luc rolled his eyes upward slightly and thought for a moment. He slowly sipped on his vodka and silently offered Kate one, waiting for her to accept. 'Tell me, you were how old when you lost . . . *it*?' he asked as he handed her the drink.

'It?' Kate replied. 'What it?'

'It.' He made a slightly vulgar motion with his fingers. 'Your flower.'

'Oh. Well, my flower is really none of your business,' Kate told him curtly.

Unscathed, Luc shrugged. 'I ask because some people, they rush to this fateful moment. Eager, thirsty, the body bursting to discover. Other people . . . well, they are the type to guard it. Like a precious gift. They wait and wait and wait.'

Kate smiled at him scornfully. She knew what he was trying to turn her into. 'You, I suppose . . . rushed.'

'Like a bull, *oui*.'

She nodded sarcastically. 'I have a picture in my head, it's very clear.'

'The picture is of a young bull, yes?' Luc asked.

'How young?'

'Thirteen.'

'Thirteen?' Kate searched for a new image of a younger Luc.

'No, you are right,' he interjected. 'I was twelve. Magda. She was a *putain*, er, a prostitute. She lived just outside the town, next to the bridge. She was . . . not beautiful. Except her eyes and her mouth. Magda's mouth, there was another world waiting there.' He stopped for a moment and sighed. 'But I had no money to kiss her, only for the fucking.'

For some reason this conversation had given him an appetite. He began to eat the cold food on the tray in front of him. It tasted like shit, but he didn't appear to care.

'I don't understand.' Kate wanted to hear more. 'Why couldn't you afford a kiss?'

'To kiss a prostitute it costs more, no matter what else. It's always been.' Luc was matter-of-fact.

Kate softened a bit. 'That makes sense.' She speculated. 'I mean, a kiss is so much more . . . intimate. You could probably disconnect from everything else but a kiss is . . . a kiss; two people's lips together, their breath, a little bit of their souls . . .' Kate was fascinated by the idea. It had never occurred to her that a kiss would be the priciest part of hired sex. It almost gave her a new respect for Luc and his whore. She leaned into her seat for a second and looked up, lost in a reverie. Sensing Luc's gaze, she remembered herself and stiffened. 'All I mean is . . . it's where the romance is, isn't it? In the kiss.'

Luc picked up on her genuine interest and sympathy. He almost detected a little spark in her heart as she spoke. He slowed down, even began to look at her a little differently. 'Yes, so I thought. Back then. The next day, I stole ten bucks from my brother Antoine. I went back to Magda. I kiss her for half an hour. It's good. Now. You.'

The plane dipped for a second and a grinding noise came from the back. Kate groaned and grabbed her seatbelt tightly, but caught herself when she saw that Luc hadn't even noticed the disturbance. She tried to collect herself. 'Me? What?'

'I tell you. You tell me. I'm all ears.' Luc looked her straight into the eye and leaned back to wait. Ten seconds lapsed.

'Okay. Okay. I didn't rush, you're right,' Kate began reluctantly. 'But I didn't hide either. I wanted it to be great. I was eighteen. Jeff the jock, in my basement, on Valentine's day.' She winced at the memory. '*Jeopardy* was playing in the background – it's a game show on TV – Jeff said it would last longer with the show on to distract him. I didn't understand why he wanted to be distracted, but by the middle of it I was the one who wanted to be distracted. And he got all of the answers wrong, too, except for sports. By Double Jeopardy we were done; by Final Jeopardy he was on his way home.'

Kate stopped for a moment and sadly reached for another little vodka bottle. She unscrewed the top and emptied it into her glass before continuing. 'That first time was bad. But since then it's been mainly good. And then I found someone special and it was great . . . Do you believe in love? The kind that lasts for ever?'

'I loved my mother,' he replied.

'Everyone loves their mother. Even people who

hate their mothers love their mother. What I want to know is: is one man meant for one woman? That's the question.' Kate watched him closely for a reaction.

Luc shuddered, as if the idea appalled him. He felt ridiculous discussing 'love' in a public place. 'But it's not an interesting question. It is the question of a little girl who is believing in fairy tales.'

'No it's not.' Kate spoke with a combination of confidence and irritation. 'It's an everyone question. And it's a question everyone thinks they have the answer to, until one day something happens and . . .' The words trailed off. Kate couldn't believe how much the vodka was loosening her up.

Luc bent towards her and looked her in the eye in an attempt to keep her going. 'Something . . . happened?'

'But I understand,' she went on, ignoring his question. 'For you, one love would be like having to eat at home every night, for the rest of your life. And you probably like to go to a different restaurant every night of the week, don't you?' She reached over and patted his little mound of a stomach. But it felt weird, not like flesh at all. She was too relaxed to hold anything back. 'Hey, what is that, what's in there?'

Luc recoiled and stiffened. '*Rien, rien* . . . it's nothing.'

It didn't occur to Kate that anyone could have something to hide on an airplane, so she smiled and playfully continued, 'What have you got in there? That's not you, you've been hiding something from me . . .'

Luc was not amused. Nor was he interested in continuing the conversation. '*Mais, arrêt.* Stop. I hide nothing.' He got up to leave.

'Whoa. Fine. Have a seat. *Pardonnez-moi.*' Kate was kind of happy that the tables had reversed. She wanted to be the relaxed one for a while.

'Okay. I will be right back . . . I must go . . .' He motioned to the toilets.

'What? You go again?' Kate was uncensorable. She was also feeling very jazzed up. She looked around for something to do or someone to talk to and found herself looking at the Perfect Passenger one seat away. She'd forgotten about him. At some point he'd put on his airplane socks and blindfold, tucked himself in with an acrylic blanket, and gone to sleep. She was impressed. She settled on a magazine and tried to become interested in it. Luc stayed away for a long time.

When Luc got into the bathroom he did not

use the toilet. He carefully pulled his sweater up and unloaded an arm-sized package. Then he pulled down the babies' changing table that was flipped up against the wall behind the toilet and gently put the package on it, the package that Kate had felt when she patted his tummy. He slowly and delicately unravelled the layers of gauze and gently laid out a fragile grapevine. It was about twelve inches long and at one end there was a clump of roots and earth, the size of a fist. Luc ran some tap water, and began to sprinkle the roots slowly. When he was sure that it had had enough to drink, he laid it back down on the water-soaked gauze. Then he pulled something out of his boot and tried to hide it in the tangle of earth and roots. It was a diamond necklace. And it looked very expensive.

By now people were banging on the door asking if he needed help. He took his time wrapping the vine up and stuffing it under his jacket before leaving the bathroom.

When Luc came back to his seat he stood for a while, looking up and down the aisles. When everything was clear he opened the baggage compartment and started shuffling around in one of the bags.

The vodka and the heat had got to Kate. She

was asleep when Luc sat back down. She should have been less trusting. He had transferred his little bundle into her knapsack.

6

KATE WASN'T SURE WHERE SHE WAS OR WHY SHE
was feeling so poorly when she woke up after the
plane had landed. Most of the passengers had already filed out of the door when Luc firmly nudged
her arm.

'Charlie?' she demanded.

'Who is Sharlie?' Luc was leaning very close
to her face.

It all flooded quickly back to Kate. The French
accent, the discomfort, the drinking and the
accusations. 'Oh.' She would have preferred
him to have disappeared before she awoke. She

wouldn't have minded never having to see him again.

'Welcome to Paris,' Luc said. He was being charming. Inexplicably nice.

She shook her head and caught a glimpse of what was outside her window. How could it be? Behind a cloudy mist she actually thought she saw the Eiffel Tower. 'Look.' She sounded hazy, and without confidence.

Luc bent down and manoeuvred himself to her window's level. 'Ah, *oui*. You will be right at home in the new France.' He sounded nonplussed.

Kate couldn't figure out where his sarcasm was coming from. She turned back to the window. She saw that the fog had thinned, and that she'd been looking at a photograph of the Eiffel Tower on a billboard for Kentucky Fried Chicken. She was deeply embarrassed, but decided to let him think that she was impressed with American kitsch. Fine. He was just an asshole that she would never see again. She filed off the plane and veered away from him on her way to the immigration lines.

After immigration she shuffled through the airport towards the baggage-claim and customs area. She rode one of the space-age escalator tubes which hung between two floors of the building. She began to look around and enjoy the strangeness of the architecture. Then she noticed that Luc was right behind her again. 'Why'd you let me drink so much?' she asked him crossly, rubbing her head to punctuate her question.

'You did it yourself.' He didn't say anything else until they got to the baggage-claim carousel. 'I give you a ride into Paris, *d'accord?* Okay, you save yourself 350 francs. Where do you stay?'

'The George Cinq Hotel, do you know where that is?'

'Wheeeew.' Luc rolled his eyes and shook his hand in a typically French gesture that looked like he had touched something that was too hot.

'Yeah. So what's all that code for?' she replied flatly.

'Well, the George Cinq, it is very *chic*, very *cher* and very *romantique*,' he answered with a shrug of his shoulders.

'Yeah. Why didn't someone tell me that a week ago?' Kate felt the humour bleeding out of her soul. But going with Luc would be easier than having to submit to another stranger, so she decided to take him up on his offer. They walked towards customs, Luc dropping back slightly behind Kate. As they went through, a bored-looking official took one look at Luc and waved him over to his station.

A flicker of resignation flashed across Luc's face momentarily. He quickly caught himself and smiled meekly at Kate. 'It is always me that they stop. I meet you outside, it will only take a minute.' He walked directly over to the stainless steel counter-top and lifted his suitcase for the inspector.

The inspector had barely begun to check him over when Luc heard a familiar voice call over to him from the baggage carousel. He turned and saw Detective Jean-Paul Cardon from the Paris police. Technically the enemy, but actually a kindred soul. Theirs was one of those affectionate cop–criminal relationships that only lawyers, judges and convicts fully understand.

Jean-Paul left his family at the baggage carousel and hurried over to the customs counter where Luc was standing. He flashed his badge at the official, acted as if something urgent was happening and hustled Luc away from the scene. The two men smiled at each other.

Jean-Paul clung to Luc's arm and moved him and his kids toward the exit door in a small controlled mass, insisting that they gave Luc a ride into Paris. When they got out to the sidewalk, Jean-Paul piled all of their luggage close to the kerb and stationed his children next to the mound so that they could flag the van down when his wife arrived from the parking lot. Luc positioned himself behind a thick cement column so that he could duck behind it if need be. He looked down towards the other exits and taxi stands, wondering what Kate had decided to do, and what he should do next. He had to get his bundle back. When the crowds finally thinned out, he spotted Kate. She was standing near the next set of doors, just twenty yards away, looking around, probably for him. But Luc knew that he couldn't bring her into the mix without Jean-Paul's curiosity being piqued. After a few more minutes, Kate gave up and flagged a taxi.

Luc watched Kate go and tried to remember everything she had said about her plans. He had to get to her before she did any unpacking.

Sitting in Jean-Paul's car hurtling towards Paris, with Jean-Paul's wife and two kids, Luc was bombarded with questions from all of them. All the while, Jean-Paul searched his bags thoroughly, but lovingly.

'You're not going to find anything in there, Jean-Paul.' Luc tried to pull his bag back and close it.

'Are you a criminal, *Monsieur*?' Jean-Paul's daughter asked him.

'Only if I'm caught,' Luc replied.

'Our Papa says that you once saved his life,' the girl continued.

'It's true, my angel,' Jean-Paul put in. 'This scar on my neck' – he tapped it – 'see it?' Of course they'd seen it. This was his basic lecture about loyalty and morality. They let him continue without interrupting. 'Luc stopped this scar from stretching from ear to ear. And he is not a criminal. I keep telling him. I hope he listens to me before it's too late. I owe him a debt much bigger than money. It is my duty to watch over him, protect him from himself.'

Luc rolled his eyes and looked out of the window. Within a moment he spotted Kate sitting in her taxi in the next lane. He was about to roll down his window when the taxi quickly veered off in the opposite direction. As he watched Kate disappear, Luc silently chanted her destination in his head. Over and over. The George Cinq, the George Cinq, the George Cinq.

7

KATE ARRIVED AT THE HOTEL FIRST. SHE WAS unprepared for the glamour and opulence that met her at the door and surrounded her every step of the way. First, two doormen in thick white gloves and morning suits opened her car door and escorted her to the heavy revolving doors. Then, another guy, in a black and red outfit, pushed the door for her so she could walk through without having to touch anything. The lobby was quiet and cavernous. There were complicated flower arrangements everywhere. Everyone was carefully dressed and put together. She suddenly felt shabby and trashy in her simple jeans and white shirt. Like she'd arrived at church in a bathing suit. Nevertheless, she marched herself straight over to the front desk. With a clear and heartfelt sense of entitlement, she rang the ridiculous gold service-bell. *Bring. Bring.*

The concierge, bald but elegant in his tuxedo, sauntered over haughtily, and let his hand fall on the bell to silence it. He looked up slowly, giving Kate the distinct impression that she neither belonged there nor deserved his attention. '*Oui, Madame?*' he offered.

Kate cleared her throat theatrically, as if to signal to him that his manner was worse than a parody of French stuffiness. 'Do you speak . . . any . . . English?' she asked sweetly.

'Of course, Madame,' he replied in perfect British English. 'This is the George Cinq, not something out of "Europe on five dollars a day".'

'It's twenty dollars a day now . . . and of course not. Could you tell me what room Charlie Lytton is in?' She got no response. 'Doctor Charles Lytton. He's expecting me.'

He sniffed, let his eyes fall on the desk-top and ran his fingers along his pencil before he replied sombrely, 'I'm afraid – *non.*'

'*Non?*' Kate wanted to throttle him.

'*Non, Madame.* Perhaps Madame could try the courtesy phone.'

Kate's eyes were bulging with anger. 'Madame has tried the courtesy phone.' She leaned forward gently and whispered, 'Do not disturb.'

The concierge came to life. He raised his hands to suggest that things were as they should be. '*Voilà*, your answer.'

People were beginning to line up behind her, but Kate wouldn't relinquish her spot until she got some kind of satisfaction. 'Monsieur. I just spent seven hours on an airplane crossing the ocean. I'm tired, I'm hungry. And I want to see my fiancé.' She pointed to her engagement ring. 'Now, are you going to help me or not?'

'Madame,' the concierge began, 'it is my duty as concierge to vigorously safeguard the privacy of our guests. And if our guests happen to need safeguarding from their own fiancées . . . well . . . After all, Madame, France is not a nation of puritanical hypocrites.'

Furious, Kate just stared at him for a moment. Was there any way to turn this guy into a human being? She decided that there wasn't, so she pulled a handful of French bills out of her pocket. After examining the pile for a moment she selected a 200 franc note, smoothed it out and placed it down in

front of him. The man managed a new disagree-
able frown as he picked up the money and folded
it into his pocket. He sniffed again, turned on his
heel and walked away.

'Hey! I just gave you 200 francs!' she called
after him, shocked.

The concierge looked at her over his shoulder.
'*Oui, Madame*, and I took it. *Merci*. If there is any-
thing else I can do to help, please let me know.'
He continued on his walk away from her.

Kate hit the deskbell very hard. *Ding*.

He stopped, visibly tensed and turned toward
her. '*Oui, Madame*, how can I help?'

'Madame would like a room,' she said with
a sarcastic smile.

The concierge didn't skip a beat. This answer
he had rehearsed and used dozens of times. 'I am
sorry, Madame, but there are no rooms.'

Kate was now out of ideas. She felt hot and
spaced-out from jet lag. Nonetheless she felt sure
that, if she waited patiently, something would happen to break her string of bad luck. She picked up
her bags and went to find someplace to wait.

As she ambled over to a large chintz sofa that
faced the elevator and the main thoroughfares, she
searched the lobby for a sympathetic face, a col-
league of Charlie's, anything that might help her

get to him. All that she found, though, were stiff, rich, young women dressed like prissy matrons, who either ignored her or stared at her blankly. Worse were the designer perfect men with brass and diamond accessories who sat in small groups, quietly murmuring to one another. She had never seen so much gold and peach and ivory silk in her life. Was it a secret aristocratic uniform? And where did they get those soft and narrow little shoes? She could have sworn that every one of them was wearing a brand new pair.

Kate sat and waited on that sofa for a long time. Mesmerised, she watched the beautiful glass elevator float up and down, in and out of view. Every time it landed she felt the same anticipation. Would Charlie be on it this time?

Feeling lost, lonely and a bit sorry for herself, she held the silver locket that was hanging around her neck. She rubbed it like an old charm and then popped it open with her thumbnail. She sat and stared at the picture of Charlie for a long time.

Looking up, she saw that a sleazy guy in a cheap, shiny black suit was watching her. Shit, she thought, he knows I'm alone and vulnerable. I'm a sleezebag's sitting duck. Shit, he's coming over. Why do I attract the scum? Why me? She could see now that he had a tiny and annoying ponytail. Yeuch.

Mr Ponytail stopped beside her and smiled a sick, seductive smile. '*Bonjour, Mademoiselle* . . . But you are an American, *non?*'

'Just for the moment.'

He figured he could sit down now, close. 'You will forgive me for intruding, but I saw you sitting here, looking a little sad. Why should such a beautiful woman as you look so sad? I asked myself but couldn't find an answer.'

'Have you got a few hours?' she answered, hoping to scare him off.

'As a matter of fact . . . Always . . .' He offered her a cigarette and continued to watch her, as if mesmerised.

Kate looked back down at the picture of Charlie in her locket, and then slowly shut it. 'Can I ask you something?'

'Of course.' He couldn't believe his luck. She was such an easy hit.

'Do you think you could urinate with someone else standing in the room, like right behind you?'

Mr Ponytail was a little taken aback. This was not what he took her for. He had to compose himself for a second before answering, 'I think I could manage it.' There was a tiny pause. 'Are you going to be the someone, by any chance?'

Kate was appalled. 'What? Me? No. Jesus that's not what I meant!' You-ask-a-scumbag-a-question, you-get-a-scumbag-answer, she figured.

But he was on a roll. 'So, you would like that I arrange for someone else to stand next to me?' He looked to her for a response but his gaze was met with a cold stare. 'It could all be arranged. Pierre . . . or perhaps you'd prefer Monique?' He decided to change course. 'You know, you have the face of an angel, but I'm delighted to find the mind is a little devil.' He smiled.

Kate had had enough. 'Okay, look,' she began. 'This is going to get you nowhere. I'm sitting here, and I'm waiting to meet my fiancé. If he sees you bothering me, if he sees . . .' Her words trailed off and her jaw fell open a bit. She was transfixed by the slow descent of the elevator.

Mr Ponytail looked to see what was getting all her attention. '*Ooh la la!*' He sounded like Gene Kelly in a musical.

Kate forgot about this annoying little man completely. Every ounce of her concentration was now back on the big, beautiful, gilt-gold elevator that was landing in the lobby. She had seen his feet first, and known immediately that it was Charlie this time. She watched as first the perfect legs, and then, the perfect torso in a tight red dress, fell into everyone's view. It was like a slow-motion nightmare waiting for the heads to finally appear. And then, yes. It was Charlie, with the most sexy and beautiful brunette, who had the biggest and iciest cat-like blue eyes she had ever seen.

Kate blinked. 'Charlie?' she murmured to herself. He looked so different. So hip and handsome. So dressed and put together. Why did his hair look so good? It was like he'd been to a decorator. She wasn't the only one staring. Everyone else around them was staring too. There was something hot and kinetic in the air. The elevator doors glided open and the pair of perfect lovers floated out, forcing the crowd around them to part. They were like movie stars. An aura enveloped them. They barely took ten steps before they had to stop. Charlie confidently turned toward the beautiful goddess, and in a single, almost choreographed motion, swept her into one of the most intense and exhibitionistic kisses in the history of French courtship. Magnets couldn't have behaved more attracted to each other.

Kate felt all of the air drawn out of the room. Then she felt all the oxygen drain out of her brain. Then she fell on the floor in a dead and heavy faint.

Charlie and the *goddesse*, whose name was Juliette, were completely oblivious to the whole thing. As half a dozen people, including Mr Ponytail, snapped out of their enchantment and crouched to help Kate, Charlie and Juliette let their lips slowly separate and, still locked in an embrace, walked through the lobby and out into the Parisian afternoon.

When Kate finally revived there was no one she recognised around, save the concierge. Charlie and the *goddesse* were gone, and even the sleazy guy with the ponytail had vanished.

As she sat up, though, she thought she saw Luc coming in through the revolving door. He talked to someone for a moment; then he looked directly at her and came right over. She was still only half conscious when she started haranguing him. 'You said you'd give me a ride, you said – hey, where are we?'

Luc talked to her like a five year old. 'Your hotel. *Viens*, come, I'll take you to your room.' He lifted her up.

Kate shook her head. It was all coming back to her now. 'I don't have a room. Someone else is in my room. Someone in four inch heels and a tight red dress that I wouldn't be caught dead in. And legs that were like . . . like . . .' She began to search the lobby around her. 'Like . . . OH MY GOD MY BAGS ARE GONE!!'

'What?' Luc had too much invested in this statement to let one reading do.

'My bags. They were right there. They're gone.' Still in shock, Kate spoke in a low monotone voice.

'They can't be gone, what does that mean, they're gone?' Luc was beginning to panic.

Kate couldn't understand what it was that he didn't get about the statement. Her bags were simply gone. She watched him scurry around like a puppy, checking behind a plant, peeking behind a counter, searching under a sofa. 'Why are you looking under there? I didn't lose my keys, someone stole my suitcases,' she said, happy that he was being hysterical for her. It let her be calm.

'*C'est pas possible!* It's – where did you put them down? Think.' Luc's voice was getting louder all the time.

'Here. Right here. I fainted over there.' Then it dawned on her. '*Oh my god, my passport, my money and my vitamins!*'

Like a fly to honey, the concierge appeared, this time accompanied by a beefy doorman. 'May I be of service?'

Luc rallied first. 'Where are Mademoiselle's bags?' he demanded.

The concierge was caught completely off-guard. 'Monsieur?'

'So you're telling me her bags were stolen from the lobby of your four-star hotel? They are just gone?' Luc was being tough. His French was getting faster and louder by the second.

The horrified concierge snapped his fingers and a small posse of bellhops ran to encircle him before they began a futile search.

'How could you let this happen?' Luc yelled, turning on Kate.

'Hey,' Kate yelled back, trying to bring him back to earth. 'What's your problem? They're my bags.'

'*Oui*, I know,' he said, catching himself. 'It's just . . . outrageous. You come to our country . . . and then . . . What do you remember? Do you remember anything from before you fainted?' Luc waited for some clues.

'No.' Kate still sounded a little confused. 'Um, some weird guy offered me a cigarette and then . . . I saw . . .' She got quiet now, even a little woozy, 'Oh, God. It was Charlie with . . .' She was trailing off into an abyss. 'You know. Men are bastards . . .'

'Not all.' Luc tried to sound sympathetic. 'Some just want to help.'

'I never thought I'd be the kind of woman to say this, but it's true, they're bastards, all of them – '

Luc tried to steer her towards specifics. 'And the man who offered you the cigarette, he was . . .'

'A bastard. A sleazy snake-in-the-grass-Euro-Armani-trash kind of a bastard.' Kate was very eloquent when she was mad.

'He was wearing a black dinner-suit, with a silk tie, *non?* He left just before I came in?' He stopped to see if she could confirm that it was who he thought it was. He had recognised the man leaving the hotel when he came in. Kate confirmed his suspicions. '*Merde!*' he swore. 'Come with me. *Viens!*' He practically pulled Kate along as he rushed towards the door.

'You know him?' She didn't wait for an answer. 'Of course you know him. All you bastards know each other.' She let herself be dragged through the lobby. As she passed the concierge's desk she felt confident about her new theory. She made eye contact with him before she spoke. 'Bastard.'

8

Luc hustled Kate through the revolving doors and out on to the street. He leaned her against the thick stone wall and after a moment's hesitation said, 'Wait here and I'll go get the car.' He hurried away down the street, surreptitiously trying the door handles on all the parked cars.

Minutes later, he confidently pulled up in front of the hotel in a new Citroën and opened the door for Kate. As he sped along the narrow streets, he explained that they were off to see someone who knew how to find the sleazy guy who stole her bags. As he talked he zipped through several lane changes, cutting in front of other cars and swerving wildly. Noticing Kate trying to apply pressure to an imaginary brake under her right foot, he sneered at her faintheartedness and drove on even faster.

Kate broke the silence, unable to sit and watch the near-collisions any longer. 'So who is he, this guy who stole my bags?'

'Bub.'

She frowned. 'What kind of name is Bub?'

'It is an American name, *comme* Bub Dylan.' Luc was short. From his clipped responses, Kate gathered that he wasn't terribly interested in talking.

'Oh, that Bub,' she said drily.

They drove over the river and careered past the Notre-Dame, passing the shimmering water and reflection without comment. Kate was too busy holding on to her seat to even notice it. As they swerved their way up past the Pyramid at the Louvre, Kate was trying to get Luc to talk again, unaware of the scene behind her. 'So this Bub. How do you know him?' She tried to sound as interested and unthreatening as she could.

'I know him from – around,' Luc said, shrugging and making a little twirling gesture with his fingers to signal that it was a small and insignificant circle that this Bub was part of.

Kate looked at him hard. 'Who are you really?' she asked.

As he rounded a corner on two wheels, Luc dug into his pocket and pulled out a small and slightly worn business card. He checked it over and then handed it to Kate. LUC TEYSSIER: BUY SELL TRADE. '*Voilà*,' he said. 'I buy sell and trade, like everybody else.'

'Not like me!' Kate told him.

'And what do you do?' Luc asked distractedly. He was having trouble keeping up his end of the conversation. He just wanted to drive.

'I'm a history teacher, grade school.' Her answer didn't even hold her own interest. She was much more interested in getting more information about Luc. 'So, why are you helping me?'

Luc put on his sincere face. 'Why? Because I like you. I do. But I don't like the way you said on the plane, with your face all scrunched up, "You're French, aren't you?" '

Kate looked down for a moment and then turned towards him. As she did so, the Eiffel Tower came into view behind her. It was beautifully lit up on an unusually clear evening. She missed it.

'I also don't like the way you say,' he continued,

'with your eyes all squinty, "all men are bastards". That hits a chord for me. I feel obliged to do something. Something big. Something gallant. Just to prove you wrong. *C'est tout.* That's all.'

Kate grabbed the sides of the car and the dashboard to hold herself up while he squealed round a corner. She lowered her foot to apply the imaginary brake again, and then asked, 'Scrunched? Squinty?'

Luc reached over, put his hand on her knee and gently pulled it back. 'Please, let me drive. Relax *toi*. Now tell me why you have come to Paris. Tell me about . . . Sharlie.'

Kate did relax a bit when she told her story to Luc. 'His calls kept getting later and later. Our conversations disintegrated. I felt like some kind of nag or something. He just sounded happier, more detached and more tipsy every day.' She frowned. Her situation was starting to sound a little peculiar, even to her. Charlie didn't come out sounding right either. She tried to correct herself, but realised that back-tracking only made things worse.

'Okay', Luc interrupted, 'I try to understand. Charlie tells you he has met a woman. No, a *goddesse*. He breaks your heart. He says he has never felt such love for anyone. He 'umilates you.'

In an effort to save face in this embarrassing scenario, Kate tried to lighten the tone and tease Luc some more. '*Humiliates.*'

'So you come to Paris to let him do it all again, this time right in your face,' he said, ignoring the correction.

'No. No, I come to Paris to get back the man I love. Is that so hard to understand and endorse?' She leaned closer to him as she spoke, willing him to support her.

Luc waved his head back and forth. 'But how? I try to imagine it. Go on, I am Charlie standing next to a *goddesse* and you are . . . well, you are you. What do you say to me?'

'I would think of something very . . . um . . . very . . . well, interesting to say.' She rolled her eyes upwards searching for an example.

'So far it is not interesting. Without something planned, something ready you would probably just start to sub.' He tapped the steering wheel forcefully to emphasise his point.

'Sub?' she asked, mystified by his English.

'You know, break down and boo hoo.'

Kate didn't give him a chance to go on. She sat up straight and cleared her throat. 'I would not "sub". I would confidently confront him. I'd be firm, but with great tenderness and feeling.'

'Meanwhile his lover is sitting back and calmly sneering at you. Very relaxed, she doesn't need to persuade or remind him of anything.' Luc mocked a sneer and leaned on the horn as they shot out into a line of traffic.

'No. No, no,' Kate said dismissively. 'Once he saw me. Myself. *Moi* . . . it would break the spell, change everything.'

Luc looked her up and down. She was a two-day-old mess. 'You won't be breaking any spells today, I think.'

'What? I could change his mind. I could. I'd remind him of our life – we had a wonderful, perfect life together.' Her voice faltered a bit.

'*Oui, bien sur.* Evidently.'

Kate was getting tired of the argument. 'We were happy. I have never been so happy. Jesus.'

'You know, whenever someone tells me they're happy, it makes my ass twitch.' Luc flared his nostrils and pursed his lips as he spoke.

Rising to his vulgar attempt at humour, Kate yelled back, 'We never fought, either. What does that do to your haemorrhoids?'

'A woman in love not fighting? Please. And my ass is fine.'

Kate tried to get back on to the subject. 'We

had plans for a home and family. I'd remind him of all of it.'

'Sure, that should work,' said Luc sarcastically, 'he was obviously very attached to these ideas.'

Kate ignored him, going on dreamily, not caring about her audience. 'And if all else failed, I'd, I'd . . .'

'You'd get down on your knees and beg?' He was a little disgusted.

Kate considered this option for a moment. 'Maybe . . .'

'*Oui.*' Luc nodded. 'Now I see it all. The *goddesse* is standing next to Charlie in her negligée, you on the knees begging. Poor Charlie. Tough decision.' As he delivered this dig, he swerved quickly round a corner and screeched into an illegal parking spot.

'If you remember, I did not beg!' Kate defiantly pulled on the parking brake and turned to get out of the car.

'No, you didn't. You fainted. Shall we go?'

Luc took Kate on a short walk through the centre of Pigalle, Paris's red-light district. Sex shops, sex bars, hookers in various costumes, states of decay or age groups, were displayed in tight doorways, crowded corners, everywhere. Beady eyes watched them as they walked. Kate ran to catch up. She saw a hooker wave to Luc in a familiar and friendly way from a doorway bathed in purple light. When she got close enough to him, she said, 'I can see how far you'd travel for the love of your life.' They reached the door of a crowded and smoke-filled café. 'After you,' she said and followed him in.

It was like a sleazy United Nations – Arabs, Africans, Asians, Europeans – everyone knew Luc and seemed happy to see him. Kate shrank a bit as Luc answered their questions and joked with them. At one point they turned to her, in unison, while he was speaking. Luc was obviously talking about her, making lewd and vulgar gestures. She couldn't believe it. He was probably claiming that he'd had sex with her. And they appeared to believe him! She waited for her moment of revenge and smiled sweetly as everyone sneaked a peek at her and chuckled.

When Luc finally turned back to her, he had changed the subject. 'My friend Abdul wants to make you his special *café*. It's black as hell, strong as death and sweet as love. An old saying.'

'Thanks but I don't drink coffee.' Luc stared at her as she went on, 'It's not good for you. Coffee, milk, it's like an assault on your immune – ' Now they were all staring. She decided to shut up. 'I'd love a cup.'

'*Bon. Un café*. Wait here, I'll be back in just a moment.' Luc slipped off and disappeared into a thick crowd at the back of the café.

Kate began to feel tired and sorry for herself. Abdul put the coffee down in front of her and everyone waited for her to drink it. She tried it, but it was unbearably strong. She smiled and pretended to like it. Before she took a second sip, a man came over to her and spoke in broken English. 'You try a French *café* and you like it. You try a French man and you like it. Maybe you try me, *non*?'

'What?' Kate caught herself. This was her chance to get back at Luc. 'Really. Now, what did my friend tell you about me? I'll tell you if it's true.' Before long they were deep in conversation. Periodically, people would wander over and join the huddle, attracted by the giggling.

Meanwhile, Luc sat down with his old friend Ali, an impeccably beautiful Algerian with dreadlocks to his shoulders. He was sitting at his usual table with a laptop opened in front of him and a modem terminal stuck into a plug in the wall, his fingers busily clicking the keys.

'Writing home to your fifteen sisters?' Luc interrupted.

Ali didn't even stop typing. 'I'm an oppressed immigrant. I have to work hard while all you fat fucks drink rare wines and eat goose liver. What do you want?'

'I'm looking for Bub.'

'You've really come down in the world. I wouldn't keep worms like Bob on my phone list.' He pretended to be engrossed in his laptop again.

Luc dug some money out of his pocket and put it on the table. '*Non?* Maybe you could just check under "w" and make sure.'

Ali turned back to him. 'You know, I'm insulted. You don't call or write for months and then you just show up and demand information. You even try to bribe me! Typical French asshole. Imperialist shit.'

When Luc handed him a little more money, Ali smiled innocently and shrugged his shoulders. 'Let's see if Chloë in Clichy is on-line, she knows where all the worms are buried.' He hunched over and got to work.

About ten minutes later, Kate saw Luc emerge from the tangle of people in the back of the café. She beckoned all her new friends to get closer and started to tell them something. She timed her punch-line perfectly. Just as Luc got close to them, they burst out laughing.

At first Luc pretended not to notice. '*Allons-y, vite*, hurry. We find him now.'

But the crowd started to hoot and holler and tease him. Kate sat back and grinned. 'Don't worry, my friend,' Abdul called out to him, 'the key is to relax.' As the laughter continued, Kate quietly took his hand and led him out of the café.

When they got outside, his jaw was stiff with anger. 'What was that?'

'Well,' Kate stepped back a bit before she continued, 'I told them that since we've been back in Paris, you know, on your home turf, that you've been having some trouble, you know . . . being a man.' She made a tiny gesture with her baby finger, like it was all limp.

Luc's whole body was stiff now. He glared at Kate for a moment and then turned on his heel and marched away quickly.

Kate went after him. 'Wait a minute, Luc. You think it was okay for you to tell them that I slept with you, but me telling them that you can't – '

He cut her off. 'Was completely, completely . . .' He couldn't find the words. He was too angry. He switched to French. '*Tu sais, il y a des limites, faut pas deconner!*'

'What's that mean?'

'To talk about a man's . . . a man's dick in front of his friends, the friends he drinks with, is . . .'

'Isn't that what guys do all the time, talk about their dicks?'

'*It's not the same!*'

'Okay, okay, I'm sorry. I missed that lesson in my Michelin Guide to France. Would that be under "French Men: Common Problems" or just under "Dicks"?'

'*It's not a problem.*'

'Evidently.' Kate couldn't believe how hard he was taking this. She tried to diffuse the tension a bit. 'It was just a joke, Luc – unless . . . You mean it's not a joke?'

By now Luc was steaming with anger. He sped along the narrow sidewalk, towards the car. Kate ran to keep up with him.

'All right, never mind. I forgive you. Let's just go.' He was practically whispering.

It was too late. Kate was on to him. 'Hey, it *is* a problem, isn't it?'

Luc tried to smooth it all over. 'No, it's nothing at all. Just a recent em . . . a recent . . . *merde*, what is the word! I've just been under so much pressure lately. Soon it passes.'

'Well!' said Kate. 'You smoke too much, eat too much, drink too much. I'm glad that there's something that you don't do too much.' She tried to imitate the vulgar gesture that he made in the bar.

'*Ça suffit!*' Luc yelled. 'Let's drop it.'

They walked in silence for a few minutes. She had no idea where the car was. Everything here was different: the sidewalks were paved in cobblestone and only eighteen inches wide in some places. Cars were parked everywhere – on corners, pathways, crosswalks, anywhere there was room for them. There were delivery cars with just three wheels, like covered tricycles. And all the shops were tiny, specialised. Kate was lost in her tired thoughts when Luc pulled her back into a recessed doorway.

'*Putain. Merde, putain, merde.*'

She searched around for whatever it was that he was hiding from and saw a swarm of policemen around the Citroën. One cop was on the radio, one was checking the plates, one was making notes and the others were standing around looking up and down the street.

Luc decided that the best way to get out of there was with purpose and conviction. He took Kate by the hand and walked right past the car. While they were still within earshot of the cops Kate spoke up boldly. 'I told you not to park there, dear.' One of the cops looked up suspiciously, but clearly hadn't understood a word.

9

KATE BEGAN WORKING ON LUC AND HIS PROBLEM
while they were on the underground metro system.
'You know,' she said, trying to get his attention,
'every man has moments like this – well, Charlie
never did, but I saw that segment on *Prime Time
Live*. It all starts with how you think about yourself.'

'Now what are you talking about?' Luc
growled.

'That you have obvious self-esteem issues,'
Kate said.

'Pah,' Luc said dismissively. He would do

anything not to have to talk about things like self-esteem. He shook his head slowly, dreading what was coming next.

Kate ignored his slight. She just pressed on with her point. 'Only a person with low self-esteem would treat his body the way you do. You need to see it as some kind of spiritual repository before you can expect to get rid of that little problem.' Kate looked him right in the eye and smiled sincerely.

'Okay,' Luc said. 'That's it. *Arrêt*. Stop. No self-help, growing, changing bullshit for me, please. Save it for your Charlie.'

They were back up on the street now, in a quiet neighbourhood behind the Sacré Coeur. Kate wasn't paying attention to any of it, though. She wanted to finish the conversation.

'So what are you saying? That you don't think that people can grow, you don't think people can change?' She wouldn't let him ignore her.

Luc rolled his eyes. 'Plants grow. The weather changes. People stay the same. Except perhaps the Americans, they are so full of their own, em, fertiliser.'

'Ha, ha, ha.'

He led her into an old apartment building. They began climbing an ancient, tight, stairway, quickly developing a hard, steady pace, as though there was a long way to go. 'Luc, look,' Kate said in her most reasonable tone, 'even though, at first glance, you are a strikingly rude and immature schmuck, I believe that underneath it all you are probably a good guy.'

'Thank you. But, no, I'm not.'

'Yes you are. You're helping me out for no good reason – '

'Look. Don't kid yourself. I'm not a good guy. Don't try to think that I'm a good guy.' Luc rolled his eyes in disbelief.

'There,' she said, misreading him again, 'see? Do you see what you're doing? Putting yourself down. That's why you have this problem.'

Luc couldn't believe what a naïve and earnest little idiot she was turning out to be. He hated this American new-age stuff. How was he going to get her to shut up? 'Okay, you are right,' he said, deciding to just give in. 'I am a terrific guy, a wonderful guy. Suddenly it is all clear to me. My self-esteem is rising – it is soaring. Really. Now for a moment, please, just shut the fuck up.' He turned away from her, lowered his shoulder and charged at a door at the end of the landing. He hit it with a thud and crashed right into the apartment.

Kate was dumbfounded. She had never known

it was actually that easy to break into someone's place – and might never have done so if she hadn't come with Luc. She followed him into a sad and empty little room, which hadn't been painted or tended to in years. A wiry guy was sitting in the centre of the room on a lone chair, wearing only a pair of pale blue boxer-shorts and an undershirt. When Kate looked closer, she realised that it was Mr Ponytail from the hotel lobby. So this was Bob. The slimebucket had been after her bags all the time.

'Bub, how are you?' Luc was talking fast, in French. 'Nice to see you, I think you've met my friend Kate, isn't that right?' He kept his eyes and body moving over the room and spotted Kate's bag. He grabbed it and started to rifle through it for his vine, first carefully and then furiously. Kate watched him toss it into the sink and move angrily towards Bob. She was totally confused by now. This was a chapter that she hadn't expected. Why was Luc going through her bag like that?

'Where *is* it? Where's everything else?' Veins were beginning to bulge in Luc's neck as he shouted into Bob's face.

'What about my money?' Kate demanded, getting into the action. 'My passport, ask him about them.'

'*Le passport?*' Bob shrugged at them impishly.

'Forget the passport,' said Luc dismissively. 'He sold the passport. That was the first thing to go.'

Kate was beginning to get anxious. 'What about my suitcase, my clothes? Ask him about my vitamins.'

'Her clothes?' he translated.

'I gave them all to Monique,' Bob mumbled quietly in French.

'*What did he say?*' Kate hated not knowing what was going on.

'He threw them away.' Luc shoved Bob across the floor and up against the wall. 'You got rid of everything? *Everything?*'

Bob meekly shook his head and tentatively pointed towards a window-sill. There it was. Luc's vine. Luc, forgetting about Bob and Kate, ran over to the little pot that the vine was resting in. He lifted it to inspect it, looked towards the heavens and kept murmuring, '*Merci, merci . . .*'

It took Kate ages to figure out what was going on. As things began to dawn on her, her anger grew. In between Luc's expressions of gratitude Bob could hear her repeating, 'Bastards . . . all of them . . . bastards . . .'

Kate collected her thoughts. Then she bolted. She snatched up her bag and left. She didn't know where she was going, or what she would do next, but she had to get out of there, away from him. The lying, two-faced bastard. How could she have let herself be duped by such a person. She must have spent too much time in Canada. She'd lost her edge, her ability to tell an asshole from a plain schmuck.

Luc, when he realised Kate had left, gave Bob one last shove and ran off to catch her. He didn't know why, since he'd got what he needed: it was some automatic pilot thing. He caught up with her on the street and kept pace as Kate launched into a tirade.

'You get me drunk. You lie to me. You put me into international legal jeopardy. You actually hide contraband in my bag. You sneak a plant in my bag, and pretend to be my friend to stay close to it . . .'

'It's not just a plant. It's a vine. A very fine vine.' Luc was half proud, half contrite.

'And that's why you were helping me, that's the only reason . . . you didn't give a shit about me, about anything but your smuggling scheme.' As everything added up and the full impact of his selfishness hit her, her rage mounted. She stepped towards him and took a swing, aiming for his chest, where the vine was.

'Hey.' Luc backed away in time. 'It's too bad that you lost all your stuff, but it was not me who stole it – '

'Right. You're practically innocent. And what would have happened if I'd been stopped at customs?' Kate asked, still boiling mad.

Luc rolled his eyes. 'Don't be ridiculous. People like you, they don't stop. Why do you think I chose you? Look at you, you would declare a pack of chewing gum.'

Kate filled her chest with a short and deep snort of air. She stared at him momentarily and then let out a commando's cry. She lunged at him. But this time she was luckier and got hold of the vine. She tugged on it until Luc began to freak out. He grabbed her wrist and forcefully prised her off.

'*Ow!*' Kate was hurt.

'*Never. Jamais plus.* Never, ever again. Do not touch my vine!' he roared. He stroked the plant protectively. 'Are you all right?' he asked, calming down.

'I'm fine. But stand back. Don't come near me.' She held her hands up rigidly, to block his advance.

'I'm not just a creep and asshole. Please understand, this vine, it is my dream, my future. Do you understand?' Luc was actually trying to get through to her. 'I will make a great vineyard one day. And it will be with this vine. This vine will get me out of this shithole.'

'Oh, donnez-moi un break, Luc. Excuse my vulgarity, but assholes like you belong in shitholes, and you can't make a whole vineyard out of this one vine.' Kate was sneering at him now.

And all Luc's passionate explanations, that of course one vine could not generate an entire vineyard, but that he knew a grafting technique that would allow him to have enough vines in just a few years to put out a small vintage, that he had a vineyard picked out to buy, he even knew exactly who he would hire to run the château, didn't make a dent in Kate. 'Look, I don't care,' she interrupted, '*I do not care.*' She waited for him to come to a full stop. 'Don't tell me about your dreams, I couldn't care less. Besides, it's bullshit, you're just a loser.'

'*Ah, oui?*' For Luc an insult was just a point of inflammation and take-off. 'And what about you? Why don't you just go home and find yourself a sweet little boy you can boss around. Only be careful you don't let him out of your sight for even two minutes. And better keep all goddesses out of his sight altogether.'

'And exactly how am I going to do that? I

don't have a ticket, I don't even have a passport.'
She noticed that he was moving towards her again.
'Don't!' she barked.

But Luc was just trying to dig through his
pockets and offer her some money. 'Here,' he
said, 'take this.' He saw in her movements that
she wasn't going to take it. 'It's yours. It's what
he got for your stuff.' He tried to push it gently
into her hand.

Kate threw back her hands to get out of his
range. 'I don't want your money,' she exclaimed
angrily. She snatched it from him and threw it up
in the air, scattering it over the street. Then she
turned away. 'Now leave, just get out of here.'

'*D'accord.* Okay, but remember, I tried – '.

Kate wouldn't let him continue. '*Go.*'

With that Luc left, walking off in one direction
as Kate shuffled off in the other. It was late now,
and the streets were mostly empty. It was Kate
who turned round and came back. She slowly
picked up the bills that were drifting on the street
and sidewalk. When she thought she had collected
them all she stuffed them into her knapsack and
left. She didn't look back again.

10

KATE SPENT HOURS WALKING THE STREETS, trying to work out what she should do. She had never felt so helpless and out of control in her whole adult life. She had never had to rely on strangers, ask favours or feel like a nameless nobody in a line-up of people looking for their lost dignity. She had always been the one that gave the help. How was she going to get back into that position?

She walked and walked and walked. It was getting late now; all the shopkeepers had locked up their stores. Only a very few fashionable restaurants seemed to have any life in them. The streets were quiet and beautiful. Kate noticed that if she walked at a certain speed, and with a heavy heel, the atmosphere matched her mood exactly. Tired, brittle and old.

She soon found herself in the centre of a little square. She stood by an old fountain and watched a wedding party pile out of several taxis in front of a beautiful little café. She was astonished at how distant she felt from the spirit of the group, how far she had come from being soothed by the image of a white wedding. Yet she couldn't help feeling moved by it all.

As the crowd went into the café and found tables overlooking the square, Kate walked over to one of the cabs they had vacated. She made eye contact with the driver before she opened the door and got in. As she sat down inside the smoke-filled cabin she enunciated, '*Embassy Americaine, s'il vous plaît.*' Nothing happened. She looked into the rear-view mirror and saw that the driver was coolly staring at her. She repeated, '*Embassy Americaine.* United States? You know *em-bas-sy?*'

The driver stared at her for another five seconds, then suddenly shrugged his shoulders. He acted as though Kate had omitted some giant chunk of polite conversation or information. Then he put his car into gear and took off. He drove wordlessly and meticulously.

By the time Kate got to the embassy, it was getting late. She'd been wandering for hours and the embassy, of course, was all locked up. Kate found herself a place near the large iron gates and sat down to rest. After about an hour, and for the first time in her life, she fell asleep out in the open, on a city street, with only her knapsack to rest on. Before she nodded off she marvelled at how her free-fall into virtual derelicthood had bothered her so much less than she'd always thought it would. She had spent so much time and energy warding off chance and disaster, and now she was finding that the dread of it was much more time-consuming and vexing than the events themselves. It was quite simple. She'd wake up in a few hours, be the first in line, get into the embassy and get her passport duplicated. Then she would figure out what to do next.

When Luc left Kate on the quiet Paris street the night before he did so with reluctance and guilt. He had used her. She didn't even know the extent to which he had put her in danger of deportation and arrest. And he'd sort of liked hanging out with Kate; there was something funny about her.

Underneath all of her typical American obsession with health and safety, she had a keen sense of humour. But she was a pain in the ass too.

Now that he had his vine back, Luc's primary goal was to get it stabilised and growing again. He walked along for a while, looking back once or twice to see if Kate had changed her mind. When he was sure he was alone, he sat down on the curb and unwrapped the vine, taking great care to examine the roots. He kept poking at them, expecting to fish out his other major treasure, but every time his fingers dived in, they came out the other end. There was nothing else in there! He became frantic, and ripped the cloth off of the plant altogether. He examined everything. The diamond necklace was not there. He felt a strong and primal roar start deep in his gut. He let out a scream like he had never done before.

He thought quickly. Bob. Bob still had the necklace. The slimy little creep. Luc was going to step on his face for this one. He was back in Bob's apartment in no time. Before Bob knew what was happening, Luc had him up against the wall again. 'Where is it, you fucking worm? Where's my neck-lace?' Luc then put him into a kind of one-armed bearhug and dragged him through the apartment. The bull in him was back. Things flew, broke and cracked open and all the while Bob maintained that there wasn't any necklace.

'I didn't see any necklace. I don't have it. It must be . . . in . . . the . . . bag . . .'

Luc stopped cold. '*In the bag?*' He left as quickly as he came. Within moments, he was racing back to where he had left Kate. He should have gone with his instincts and not left her alone in the first place. When he got there, all that was left was a 50-franc note, swirling around in a tight circle of wind. It might as well have been a month ago. Grabbing the money he ran off, trying to think where to go and what to do next.

He had to keep moving – otherwise his whole future was back in the shit-hole. His natural next step was to get himself some more wheels. This time he chose a powerful motorcycle whose reckless and trusting owner had used a simple bicycle lock for security. He had the lock opened and the bike started in two minutes. That was just one minute less than the owner had needed to go into a nearby *tabac* and get some cigarettes. Luc was taking off down the street when he heard the screams of the guy chasing him. As he rode away, Luc wondered why people did that. Was it because they saw it in the movies or was it because they honestly thought that a thief would stop for them?

Luc's only good idea was to go back to the George V Hotel and hope to find Kate or some tentacle that would lead to her.

At the American Embassy, Kate had fallen into a deep and restful sleep that lasted much longer than she'd thought possible. When she awoke it was 8.20, the sun was high in the sky and the streets were alive with cleaners, pedestrians and delivery people. Kate saw that the line-up to get into the embassy had already grown long and impatient. At exactly 8.30, a Marine opened the gates and let the people file up the stairs into the offices. Kate slowly got up and took her place in line.

She had to wait for about an hour before she was directed to the window of a very officious and unyielding woman wearing a tight US marine uniform.

'So how long do you think it will take? The rumour in the line was that it usually takes a couple of days to get a new passport.' Kate used her cajoling voice. It didn't work.

'I see that you are currently a resident of Canada. That you are in the process of applying for Canadian citizenship.' Sergeant Kuhn had a ring of judgement in her voice.

Kate smiled a big goofy smile and said, 'Well,

my fiancé is Canadian.' She wondered if female subordination would score any points.

'Let me ask you something.' Kuhn was unimpressed. 'You no longer want to be an American, but you expect me to give you a new passport?'

'Is this a trick question?' Kate answered, wondering if Kuhn had the discretionary power to weed out Americans that weren't patriotic and gung-ho enough. She decided that power was, by definition, discretionary and that Kuhn could therefore use any number of excuses to torture her.

For the first time, Kuhn looked up at Kate. She smiled flatly. 'I'll need a copy of your Canadian resident visa before I can process your application.' Then she looked over Kate's shoulder to the next person in line and said, 'Next.'

Kate was flabbergasted, yet unsurprised by the treatment she had received. Everything had gone wrong since that phone call from Charlie came in. Why should things begin to right themselves now? She'd never been on a downward spiral, but deep down she knew that this was a ride that she'd probably have to take to the very end of the line. The bottom. She couldn't believe it. Everyone was treating her like a scruffy loser. She began to think about all the platitudes she'd heard in old movies and books about how having nothing makes you needy and being needy makes you undeserving. It was a profound revelation. Once you slip out of the circle of entitlement, it becomes impossible to get back in. And if you're out there it must be because you deserve to be.

She decided to go on to the Canadian consulate. She allowed herself two emotions. One that they would somehow, miraculously, see through all of her dirt and bad luck and realise that she really was a sweet, deserving and wrongfully excluded member of their club. Her second, simultaneous feeling was that she should just go on with her odyssey until it was over. According to the cliché, she would have to hit bottom before things would get better again.

The line at the Canadian consulate was longer and its members more politely behaved. This she expected and welcomed. The Canadian guards were just as authoritative in their behaviour, but much goofier in demeanour, and the civilian employees seemed friendlier and less harassed. She let herself relax slightly in the clean, well-kept building. From the tall and seriously decorated foyer she could see into the sombre office areas, lined in mahogany panelling, and the calm officiousness of the Canadians made her feel that everything was going to be okay.

After about an hour, she was directed to a large, dark, wooden desk and invited to sit down opposite a young man who was so comfortable-looking that she almost addressed him as a friend. His name-plate said Scott Campbell, he wore an almost hip-looking single-breasted grey suit and had a round and happy face. She was so relieved by the sight of him that she began to let her guard down.

After a few polite interchanges about being a 'Canadian' in Paris, Mr Campbell moved into a more business-like tone. He had a sweet Canadian accent that made everything sound like a question. 'So how it works is, I ask you a question? And then you make a comment?' Kate moved in closer to him and nodded.

'So, you weren't supposed to leave Canada, eh?'

Kate collected herself, even though she felt like her luck was changing and she was going to sail through this one easily. 'I know that,' she said, 'I do. But an emergency situation arose and I needed to . . .' She stopped when she saw him scribbling something down in the open file. She tried to stay calm. 'What was that you just wrote down?'

Campbell glanced up at her and blinked before

he continued. Suddenly he seemed very eager to play the bureaucrat. 'Why didn't you request permission to leave for this emergency? There is a procedure for that.'

'Yes I know, and I should have. But an emergency, by definition, doesn't really give you the time to go through all the . . .' She felt that she was losing him. She decided to change her tactics. 'Look,' she started again, 'the thing is, I want to be a Canadian more than anything. I want to be just like you. Canada is my home. Believe me. I just want to go back home.' At first she thought she was making some headway with him. He smiled, blushed and nodded. Then he became distracted for a moment and started to read one of the papers in the file intently. Kate tried to see what it was, but couldn't. 'What's that?' she asked.

'Oh. Uh huh. Ya,' Campbell said nervously. He looked up. 'Have you ever been convicted of a felony?' He spoke very deliberately, with his eyebrows raised way up.

They locked in a glance for a long time before Kate spoke. She opened her mouth and started to move her lips like she had just learned to speak. 'No?' she whispered in Campbell's direction.

Campbell ran his eyes across the page again before he stared at her and wrinkled his forehead knowingly. Kate had no choice. 'Yes. Okay.' She let the whole story out in one confessional breath. 'I was at this party at Ronnie Templeton's house. Someone passed me a cigarette. I thought it was . . . okay, I knew it wasn't just a cigarette. It was . . . peer pressure. Peer pressure is a terrible thing when you're a girl in college . . . You know?'

Campbell nodded ominously. He still spoke as if everything was a question. 'We just received this letter. From a Sergeant Kuhn at the American Embassy. It says that you were once convicted for possession of a narcotic?'

'Now, is marijuana really a narcotic?' she asked beseechingly. He shrugged his shoulders affirmatively. She went on, 'Look, it was just the one time. I didn't even enjoy it. I mean I inhaled, but then I started to cough and cough. I was going on for about ten minutes.'

Campbell broke into a grin of familiarity, almost camaraderie. 'Oh yeah. I hate that.'

Kate leaned forward in amazement. 'You do? Really?'

Campbell realised he'd been charmed and almost seduced by Kate's colossal cuteness, and that he'd gone too far. He pulled himself and his heart way back into a bureaucratic shell and sighed. 'The point is, Miss Taylor, you didn't include this information in your application for Canadian citizenship, paragraph 5, article 1?' His tone suddenly became apologetic. 'This is where I have to tell you that your request for a new residence visa has been denied.' He grimaced sympathetically and let a big rubber stamp fall hard on to the pile of paper in front of him. Thump.

Kate tried to smile. She could only come up with a quiet and unconvincing, 'Thank you?' before she fell into the back of her chair. She could barely grasp the enormity of her bad fortune. Was this the bottom? Was there more horror and humiliation around the next corner? Was this Charlie's fault or did she only have herself to blame? Is this why people suddenly became religious? Did she have any more options available to her? Would she have to go and camp out in Charlie's hotel and beg for a loan and some sympathy? She resolved that that would be the last thing she'd do. She wanted to get back on the street and start moving. Something would come to her if she just kept moving.

11

IT WAS WAY PAST NOON WHEN KATE GOT BACK into familiar territory. She shuffled past the Chanel, Christian Dior and Armani shops wearing her three-day-old jeans and white shirt. She tried to devise ways of getting back her status, both as a worthy human being and as a woman who was meant to be happily married in a few short months.

Although Kate couldn't help feeling that the general environment was malevolent and cold, she was continuously struck by the charms and beauty of the Parisian streets. She'd turn a corner and find an old and beautiful cobble-stoned square, filled with life and light. Or she'd stumble upon an open-air market that looked as though it had been taking place since the seventeenth century: old ladies selling huge bundles of fresh-cut flowers, fishermen in ancient navy costumes sorting through heaps of fresh scallops, oysters and clams. Her sadness was both sharpened and sweetened by the poignancy with which she experienced these sights and sounds and the fantastic differences from her own life. She longed for Charlie to be at her side so she could share it all with him.

By two o'clock she was tired and hungry and lost. She re-counted the handful of money that she'd got from Luc and decided to spend what she had to for a decent lunch. About to join a long line at a pastry shop where she could buy a simple sandwich, she caught a glimpse of the Eiffel Tower reflected in the large, plate-glass window of an expensive and chic restaurant. She turned round in circles in a vain attempt to see the real thing. It had to be there somewhere. If it was reflected in the window, it had to be! She ran her eyes over every vista, roof-top and street in sight. The tower was not there. However, when she turned to see the reflection in the window again, she found a different sight.

A waiter had pushed open the glass window to let in the afternoon air and sunshine. As he did, he revealed the restaurant interior, filled with smartly dressed people with perfect posture. It took about three seconds for Kate to realise that someone very familiar was in her field of vision. Charlie, dressed in a funny beige suit and gaudy dress-shirt, was feeding a sexy woman in a spaghetti strap dress with a parfait spoon. It was the fucking *goddesse* again, and she was relishing every bite.

Kate had nothing left to lose. She did not cry, she did not swoon. This time she got mad. Charlie was not going to stay with this sex kitten. He was going to come home and start again with Kate. Just as she was about to force her way into the restaurant and boldly stride over to their table, she caught a glimpse of herself in the glass that she'd seen the Eiffel Tower in a few moments before. She looked awful. She was sloppy and dirty and jet-lagged. Next to the sex kitten she looked like a pathetic, scorned has-been. She decided that she would confront them later, after she'd found a way to restore herself. As she stepped away, she froze in horror as she spotted something big and shiny on the *goddesse*'s ring finger. Oh my God! she thought. They think they're engaged.

It was time to phone home. Kate found an empty phone booth on the Champs-Elysées and placed a collect call to Charlie's parents' house. Her soon-to-be sister-in-law Lilly answered the phone.

'Tell me what's going on, Lilly. I saw a ring on the girl's finger.' Kate was quick to the point.

'Yeah. I know. He proposed to her.' Lilly spoke in her affected, urban-sophisticate voice. 'What an asshole. I can't believe you're not going to be my sister any more. Do I have to be friends with Juliette? God, is that really her name?'

'Lilly, stop it. He's not going to marry her. Now, tell me everything you know.'

'They're going somewhere in the south of France to meet her parents. Then they're going to get married, before they even come back to Toronto,' Lilly sounded disgusted. 'Not that I'd go anyway.'

Although this confirmation of her suspicions made her feel faint, Kate pressed on in a business-like tone. 'Lilly, listen, this is very important, very important. You have to tell me exactly where they are going and when. Ask mom, she'll probably have it all written down.' She rested her elbow on the small shelf in the booth to steady herself.

'Okay, but are you still supposed to be calling her mom?' Lilly couldn't let discretion overrule her ghoulish curiosity.

Kate lost her cool. '*Lilly!*' she snapped. 'Go. Ask her now. Quick.' She looked around while she waited and noticed that she was only about fifty yards from the Arc de Triomphe. As she thought about her own possibilities of losing and triumphing she started to feel very sad and sorry for herself. By the time Charlie's mother got to the phone, she was crying.

'Hello, Kate? Is that you sweetheart? Kate, I think you can still get Charlie at the hotel in Paris. I don't think he's left yet. Kate? Are you crying? What did Lilly say to you, dear?'

Kate felt pathetic and embarrassed. She tried, unsuccessfully, to talk normally. 'No, mom, it's okay, I'm not crying. It's just that I'm going to get him back. I'm going to win him back and make him love me again. We're going to live happily ever after, mom. I'm gonna win him back. I am. Thanks mom. I gotta go now. See you.' Kate sniffed quietly and hung up the phone, dried her eyes and tried to shake herself into a tough, confident stance. Then she strode bravely up the boulevard beyond the Arc and on to the hotel.

Back at the hotel, everything looked serene and rich. She walked into the lobby and searched out her friendly concierge. She had no idea that the theft of her bags had sparked a serious police investigation.

She was, therefore, also unaware that Bob was being questioned in the manager's office at that moment. He had been caught by Luc's buddy from the airport, Detective Jean-Paul Cardon, while trying to snatch a purse from another hotel guest. So without knowing it, almost everyone she had met in France was in the hotel with her – everyone except Luc.

Kate decided she wouldn't leave the hotel until she got exactly what she wanted. As she moved through the lobby, she also decided that the old rules didn't apply any more. Rude would be met with ruder. Sarcastic would be met with shrewder. Belittlement would be met with total indignation. She looked around to size up her audience, planted herself at the front desk and dropped her hand once, with determination, onto the desk-bell. *Ding!*

When the concierge finally looked up and recognised her, she put on a big, sweet grin and said, 'Hi there, *c'est moi*. Little old me.'

The concierge twitched, amused at the prospect of being bitchy to a naïve American again. 'Welcome back, Madame, to the George Cinq.' He was smooth.

Kate smiled and nodded her head knowingly. 'It's incredible how you do that. The words come out of your mouth, "Welcome back Madame," but the meaning is completely different. What's the deal, is that a French thing, or just a concierge thing?'

The concierge lifted an eyebrow languidly. 'As Madame wishes.' He made English sound like a vulgar chore.

'There, you did it again. It's something I'm learning here in your country, how to express hostility in a low-key, ultra-superior kind of way. You see, at home, if I wasn't getting good service, like if some creep was giving me grief about what room my fiancé was staying in, I wouldn't be as subtle, or as ironic. I'd just lose my temper. I'd scream my head off or something. Like this.' She stepped back and began to pound the desk-bell over and over. The entire lobby came to a stop. Every eye was on them and she was still pounding. When she was sure that everyone was paying attention, she stopped. 'Ah. That felt good.'

The concierge was more than a little unnerved. 'Thank you, Madame, for the fascinating lesson in our cultural differences.' He looked around, waiting for people to return to their own business. 'I'm sure it would not betray my duty to inform you that your fiancé and his, shall we call her friend, are no longer our guests.'

'Oh, and whose guests might they be now?' Kate gave him a moment to answer. When she saw the smug smile return to his tight lips she raised her hand, ready to begin pounding the desk-bell again.

The concierge covered the bell with his own hand and began to talk. 'The Carlton Hotel in Cannes will have the happy privilege when they arrive in the south of France tomorrow.' He let his smooth tone return as he continued, 'Perhaps Madame wishes to catch the last train tonight out of Paris? I could arrange for a taxi immediately.'

Kate triumphantly accepted the doorman's courtesies and jumped into a sleek beige taxi in front of the hotel. She did not notice a motorcycle pulling up behind her as she drove away. Luc jumped off the bike and ran into the hotel.

Throughout Kate's little episode in the lobby, Bob was sitting in the manager's office behind a one-way glass, being interrogated by Jean-Paul.

'Come on, Bob,' the inspector was saying, full of clichés, 'you must know how it works. If the little fish wants to survive in the pond, he must tell the fisherman where to find a bigger, better fish for his dinner.'

At first Bob held out, honourably quiet. He would not give up any of his comrades to save himself. Besides, once you'd informed on someone, it would become impossible to continue in the criminal community. 'Forget it,' he said, 'I'm no rat.' He tried to concentrate, even when he spotted Kate and his adrenalin started to pump wildly. When he figured out that she couldn't see him through the one-way glass, he relaxed. He decided to hold his ground until they gave up on him and let him go. Then he saw Luc charge into the lobby and he quickly changed his mind. He could kill two birds with one stone. He could get back at Luc for busting up his apartment and he could get the inspector off his case.

He watched Luc lift the concierge over the front desk by his lapels. 'Okay,' he said to Jean-Paul, 'I give you . . . your pal. Luc Teyssier. He just got back from the States, *non*? Ask him about a stolen necklace. He's right behind you. Over there.'

As the inspector turned to look, Luc raced from the hotel lobby. He had prised the information he needed about Kate from the concierge. So when Jean-Paul came out of the office, the concierge had only to say 'Gare de Lyon. The night train to Nice,' before the cops jumped into their cars and sped off in pursuit of Luc. Now there was an entourage following Charlie to meet his in-laws.

The scene at the station was like a French farce. Luc arrived in a total panic. The station was filled with commuters and travellers. Kate, in her navy jacket and jeans, would be practically indistinguishable in this crowd. He checked all the people gathered under the information and timetable boards first. Next he strode quickly up and down the ticket lines. Then he pushed past a few clumps of teenagers and saw her, standing in a line, waiting to be abused by a ticket agent. He wiped the sweat off his face and tried to steady himself.

Kate's back was to him. The bag was dangling off the tip of her finger, down her back. It was fairly clear all around her. It was as good a time as any to approach. He quietly moved closer. Just as he reached for the bag, Kate turned round, her ticket in her hand. Luc didn't skip a beat. He immediately put on a big smile and kept his arm extended, as if to touch her in greeting. His hand caressed her bag and her back as he gently directed her towards the departure lanes.

Kate was so tired by now that nothing surprised her and nothing scared her. She shook her head, trying to hold back an exasperated laugh. 'What do you want?'

'I've come to make peace with your people.' She walked away from him. He tried to catch her up. 'You're still after your Sharlie, *non*? You are *incroyable*, inspiring. I really admire your persistence, it is so American of you.' He had on his most slimy and charming voice.

'Correction. I'm not an American. I'm a soon to be ex-American Canadian.'

Luc concentrated on the bag. 'Can I help you with that?' She jerked it away from him. 'Well, perhaps not,' he continued. 'You know, Kate, I'm feeling some very strange emotions for me. Like never before. I'm feeling guilt. Remorse. My self-esteem, as you call it, is rock bottom. I just want to say I'm sorry. I want to make it up to you.'

'Oh, please,' she said flatly, 'you haven't spent sixty seconds with me when you weren't after something. What is it now, Luc, buy, sell or trade?'

Luc flashed a contrite smile at Kate and strode alongside her as he tried to explain. '*C'est vrai*, it's true. I used you, a lot.' His eyes darted nervously around, looking for a place to escape to when he snatched her bag. 'You helped me with my vine and I left you with nothing. So, now I ask myself,

Luc, what can you possibly do to make it up to her?' He dropped behind her, reaching for the bag. 'So now I am here – ' His speech trailed off as he spotted Jean-Paul and his lackies. It was clear that they were after him. He forgot the bag and took off in the opposite direction.

Kate looked around and saw that Luc was gone again. She was not surprised. She just shook her head in mild disgust and continued on her way, unaware that she was leading a crook and a team of cops through a slapstick, train-yard routine. The inspector and his assistants were chasing him, climbing, searching and bullying without elegance or efficacy.

At the last moment, Luc spotted Kate's train as it was pulling out of the station two tracks away. As he jumped the tracks and hopped on to the train he saw Jean-Paul calmly watch him get away from across the tracks. Luc signalled to the inspector in friendly respect before disappearing into the moving train to find Kate.

12

Luc sat down beside Kate in the train compartment and continued on as if he had never left her side. 'I ask myself what can I possibly do to make it up to you? So I buy this train ticket' – he held up a fake ticket – 'and here I am, for you . . .'

'Ssh. Be quiet.' Kate wasn't paying any attention to him. She was staring out the window, amazed at what she saw. It was the Eiffel Tower, tall and elegant, rising above the Seine. She savoured the sight. When the tower disappeared she turned back to Luc. Now there wasn't a tense bone in her body. 'You come, you go, you promise one thing and deliver another. The bullshit just never ends, so why should I believe anything you say?'

'I have no reason to lie any more,' he replied, trying to sound convincing. 'Do I look like the kind of a guy, who would leave Paris just to bullshit a stranger?'

'You look like the kind of guy who steals the little liquor bottles they serve on airplanes. You look like the kind of guy who offers a girl a ride and then has to steal the car to give it to her. The kind of guy who smuggles a vine in some-one else's bag . . .' Kate spoke quietly but with confidence. It was clear from her voice that she no longer expected any help from him or anyone else.

'Okay, *arrêt*, stop. I get the picture.'

'So, how did you find me?' Kate watched him consider the question. He pulled out a cigarette and lit it. 'Hey, hey, this is a no-smoking compartment.' Suddenly she realised that she didn't care about rules any more, or about smoking. 'Oh, forget it. Just open the window.'

Luc's face brightened. 'You see? For you, change is like growth. We help each other, *non*?'

'I don't need your help.' She smiled mockingly.

'Oh, *non*? So tell me, do you have a plan now for your Charlie?' He waited momentarily for an answer, but he could tell that none was coming. 'Ah, still *non*. You are engaged in battle and you have no armour, no strategy. No . . . bullshit.'

'I don't need bullshit to get Charlie back.' She was aloof.

'Oh, really? And when you arrive in Cannes, what will you say to him? Are you planning to be indignant? *Non*, a bad idea, I think. You could play it, eh, very cool, that would be better. And what will you be wearing? That?' He leaned over to her and touched her lapel. 'Kate, for me, making up bullshit is like breathing. It's easy and it's necessary. You need me for ammunition. So I stay, I help. I promise you I will. Okay?'

Kate couldn't believe she was still talking to this sleazeball. 'Do what you want. It's a free country. Or is it?'

Luc was relieved. He could stay and get another pop at her bag. He just sat back, relaxed, and waited for his next opportunity.

Miraculously, no new travellers came into the compartment to disturb their quiet, slightly fragile truce. That night, after hours of watching the countryside, things became relaxed between them. Kate leaned into the corner of her seat and began to play with her locket. She'd been daydreaming for some time when she absent-mindedly opened it and smiled at the two tiny pictures of Charlie inside.

Luc leaned in. 'Is that him? Can I, uh . . . ?' He took her small nod as a 'yes' and quickly shifted into the seat beside her to take a good look. He moved a little closer than he needed to. 'How did you meet?' he asked.

She smiled at the memory. 'At a party. I was in Toronto for work. We just started talking and I got this feeling about him. It wasn't exactly like a thunderclap, or lightning bolt, it was more like a . . .' She hunted for the right word.

'Like a light drizzle?' He couldn't talk about love seriously.

Kate was short. 'You really honestly never have had that feeling about someone in your whole life? Honestly?' She hated the fact that he mocked not only her corny statement, but her beliefs, her good faith and her basic attitudes about life.

'I would not admit a feeling like that if I did.' He pointed at one of the pictures of Charlie and said, 'His chin looks a little weak. If you ask me.'

'No it doesn't, and I didn't ask you.' She was sorry she ever loosened up and confided in him at all. 'Why wouldn't you admit a feeling like that?'

'Why should I admit such feeling? Look where it has gotten you.' When he looked up, his eyes were only a few inches from hers. He felt a slight and unexpected shudder.

'Well, it sounds like we're getting somewhere here.' It was her turn now. 'Maybe if you did admit such feeling you wouldn't have that little problem we don't like to talk about.' She caught his eye and looked down at his crotch.

'It's not a problem. It's just a temporary . . . phase.' Luc tried to change the subject again by pointing at the locket. 'You know, there is something in his eyes. Vain, is it a word?'

'It's a word.' She was a little surprised by his viciousness. 'And he has beautiful eyes.'

'*Oui*, and he clearly knows it. You can see it in the smile. Not really a smile, it's more like a . . . smirk, is it a word?'

'Yes smirk and vain are both words.' Kate closed the locket and tucked it away. She turned and added, 'Shut up, is it a word?'

'Two words, *non*?' he ventured. 'Now. Why are you chasing after him, after what he's done to you?'

'I love him. It's either Charlie or no one. Ever again. I don't think I'll ever be able to want anyone, ever again.'

'You say that now. But in time you would forget. First you'd forget that chin, the smirk, his nose. Then you would struggle to remember exactly the colour of his eyes. And one day you would wake up and he would be gone; his face, his smell, his voice. He will have left you. And then you can begin again.' Luc spoke with quiet conviction.

Kate wasn't sure that was what would happen if she never got Charlie back. But she did get the feeling that Luc himself was talking from experience, and that his scorn for her love of Charlie was bullshit. Like everything else about him.

Exhausted, she leaned back in her seat and before long started to nod off. Every few minutes she'd jerk herself awake and remember where she was. She tried to make her bag into a pillow between her and the window, but when that didn't work she laid out along both seats and balled up her knapsack under her head.

Luc watched all this in dismay. He waited as long as he could: he wanted her to be fast asleep before he tried to get his necklace back, but he was so anxious that every moment felt like an eternity. When he finally crept down between the seats and tried to take the knapsack, Kate jerked awake and bundled the bag even closer.

About half an hour later he tried again. Kate was curled up like a cat, facing away from him.

If he could just reach in behind her head and unzip the bag, just enough to get his hand in . . . He felt around inside it for a moment, but the movement made Kate stir and shift position slightly. Luc froze. He was stuck. *Merde*. Shit. He tried to wriggle his hand free and get into some of the outside pockets, but when he looked for a place to rest his free hand to brace himself with, he found himself mesmerised by her body. Why hadn't he noticed how nice it was before?

He had to ignore it completely and proceed. He didn't want to think about her physically. But when he dug into the bag again, she rolled over on to his arm, landing with her face just inches away from his. Now he was pinned down. He could feel her breath falling on to his chin. Kate nudged closer with such familiarity that he was sure she was doing it on purpose. She mumbled something about Charlie. Then she started kissing him.

At first Luc tried to resist. He felt like an actress in an old James Cagney movie. Then he let himself get into it; he relaxed and the kiss became deeper and more passionate. Exciting.

Kate pulled back and rested on her arm again. Luc stared at her. She actually opened her eyes for a second, smiled, sighed, and closed them again without ever waking up. Luc slumped back, astonished and dazed, completely forgetting about the necklace. Then he fell asleep and stayed asleep far beyond sunrise the next morning.

13

WHEN HE WOKE AND FOUND THE COMPARTMENT
empty, his first and only thought was to find Kate.
As he raced from compartment to compartment
the thought of the necklace getting away from him
made him frantic. After a few terrible minutes he
found her sitting alone in the dining car with a huge
cheese tray in front of her. She looked like she was
eating her first meal in days.

As he approached, Kate threw him an open
and unguarded smile. It was clear to Luc that
she had no memory of what had happened
the night before. She made a friendly gesture

with her elbow, inviting him to sit down, and began to talk without stopping to breathe or swallow. 'I can't seem to get enough of this cheese. And I haven't eaten the stuff in years. Boy, you don't look like you got much sleep last night. For some reason I feel incredibly refreshed. I had this dream, I can't remember it exactly. It was one of those dreams you have sometimes that just leaves you with a delicious feeling. And when you wake up you feel sort of transformed.' She glanced at Luc and saw him staring at her blankly. Undeterred, she carried on, looking out of the window as she spread a glob of goat's cheese on her bread. 'God. It is so beautiful here.'

Luc continued to act like he was in a daze. He rubbed his eyes, checked to make sure the bag was still close by, and signalled to a waiter. '*Un café crème.*'

'Did you know that there are four hundred and fifty-two official, government-approved cheeses in this country?' Kate asked, looking up for a sign of life from Luc. She waited for an unenthusiastic nod before continuing. 'Don't you think that it's incredible to come up with four hundred and fifty-two official ways of classifying what is essentially a bacterial process?'

'And what would you prefer? One cheese? One cheeseburger to put it on? One restaurant to eat it in?' Luc growled.

Kate frowned. 'Sheesh. What side of the train did you wake up on?' Her cheerfulness was irrepressible. 'I'm saying that I like the cheese, I like the variety.' She looked back out at the exquisite countryside and repeated, 'God it is really beautiful here. I don't think I've ever seen . . . What's that face, Luc? You don't think it's beautiful here?'

'Phew. No, it's just, um . . . that . . . I was born here.'

'Really? But it's so beautiful, so serene and charming, so . . .'

'So I had to leave. Yes. Too beautiful for me.'

They stopped talking for a while and sipped their coffees while they watched the hills and vineyards roll by. Tiny hamlets or villages built in matching colours of stone and terracotta were perched on occasional hilltops or nestled in lush valleys.

Their meditative quiet was interrupted by Kate. '*Oh God.*' She bent over in spasm.

'What. What is it?'

Kate didn't answer for a long time. She rocked herself as she sat doubled over in her seat. 'I'm going to die. Oh God. Ow. Ow. Ow. Please make it stop.'

'What is it? The cheese?'

Kate recoiled. 'Don't say that word. *Oohhh*, please stop the rocking, just for a while.'

'I can't stop the rocking. It's the train.' Luc tried to offer her some water.

There was no way. Kate just doubled over in another cramp. 'Oh. Oh. Okay, this is it. Here it comes. The mucus. It's . . .'

Luc figured he should just keep talking, regardless of the subject. 'What mucus?'

'Oh man, this is killing me. It's another spasm. Yeow. I should have known this would happen. You gotta do something, please.'

'Okay. Okay, let's look out of the window together. At the cows.'

'*Not* the cows. Get me off the train. I have to get off the train.'

'*Non. Non.* Not possible.'

'You better hurry or it's going to be trouble. *Yeow.*'

14

As soon as the train pulled out of the station and the diesel fuel scent cleared, Luc could detect the calm still smells of the region. The station stood on the edge of a typical small village, a village that just happened to be near his family's farm. It had been almost ten years since he'd been back, but the aromas, the dampness of the air and the still sound of absolutely no industry, save the occasional agricultural machines, brought back whole landscapes of memories and emotions. This had not been part of the plan, and he felt vulnerable. An annoying and nosey old man wearing a railroad uniform kept badgering him about his name. 'François Gilbert? . . . Jacques Morales? . . . Phillipe Cazal? . . .' Luc just ignored him. Even when he got it right, Luc pretended that he didn't hear him.

'Luc Teyssier!' The old man ran to a phone and started to call around with the news.

When Luc saw Kate stumble out of the station WC, he asked, 'Are you okay now?'

'Better,' she replied weakly. 'When's the next train?'

'Not for another two hours.'

'Good, I need to take a walk. I've gotta walk.' Kate pushed herself back on to her feet and signalled for Luc to follow.

'No, *non, non*. That's not a good idea. We should wait quietly for the train, you should rest,' he said, hoping to stay put.

'I'm walking. I gotta walk,' she insisted.

He got up to follow her, cursing under his breath. When he turned around to check on the old guy, he saw that he was still gossiping on the phone.

Luc tried to keep them to back roads and old paths. Everything was ancient, winding and perfect. Kate noticed every detail, even as she fought with her stomach.

'I have a very sensitive stomach. Always have.
It's where I put all of my stress. God the buildings
are so . . . ow . . . ow . . . gorgeous here. How
could you be from here? You didn't really grow
up here, did you?'

Luc was glum. 'I grew up here. Yes.'

'Well you don't have to whine about it, I grew
up in Akron, Ohio. That is something to complain
about. Oh my God, my liver . . . ow . . . ow . . .
Whew, we have to get to an herbalist.'

'Oh, sure,' replied Luc sarcastically. 'The herbalist is around the corner. Coming up.'

They continued along a stone path and came
upon a group of older men talking to a young
couple. It looked like they were trying to trade
a cow for an old Peugeot. One of the older guys
did a double-take when he saw Luc. Luc decided
not to react, but the old man leaned over and
whispered something to his young grandson and
the boy took off towards the town.

'How long since you've been home?' Kate asked.

'Six years.'

'Six years! Is your family a nightmare or something?'

'Let's not talk about it.'

'You know it's a sign of good health to be
able to express things,' she told him. 'What you're

feeling, thinking . . . Express not repress.'

'Well, then, you must be the healthiest person in the world,' he said drily.

'Why are you shutting yourself off from me? Do you know what happens to people who shut everyone out?'

'They lead quiet and peaceful lives.' Luc was not prepared to give her any headway into a conversation about his family. He remained quiet for several minutes as they walked along the curved path towards town. After several minutes they found themselves in a small square with an open café in the centre. They sat down at one of the tables and ordered some drinks. As they waited, they saw the young couple who had previously been driving the old Peugeot walk through the square leading the cow by a rope. The whole scene made life in the provinces seem like a perfect pastoral time-warp, free of stress, harassment and violence.

When their drinks arrived, Kate picked up their previous conversation. 'People who shut everyone out just fester.'

'And I am festering?'

'Yes, inside. Fester and rot. Don't laugh. I've seen it happen. You'll become one of those hunch-backed, lonely old guys who sit in the corner of crowded cafés mumbling to yourself, croaking and contorted. "*Ehchh!* My ass is twitching, all you people make my ass twitch." ' She looked up at him cheerfully and threw up her hands in a gesture of liberation. 'Or you can avoid all that, right here with me. Now. Just let it out and – '

Kate's harangue was interrupted by the squeal of a black BMW convertible. The car zoomed into the square and screeched to a stop directly in front of Luc and Kate's table. Kate didn't know what to think. The only thing that came to mind was that this looked like a scene in *America's Most Wanted*.

Luc knew exactly what was going on. He jumped to his feet, charged with adrenalin, and made his way around the car towards the driver's side. As he reached for the handle, the door opened, just missing Luc, and a well-dressed, handsome man jumped out and grabbed at Luc before getting clear of the car. They spoke fiercely to each other in French.

'What are you doing here. *eh*?' the man said, shoving Luc in the chest.

Luc thrust out his lower jaw and shoved him back. 'I came. I'm here. In five minutes I'll be gone.'

'Oh no,' the guy replied as he shoved back at Luc. 'You can't just show up! That's part of the deal!'

Luc grabbed his lapels and started to tug. 'Then the deal is going to have to change.'

They began to wrestle, fumbling and tripping over each other's feet. Luc would try to push his opponent to the ground and would end up twirling around with him before they both fell. The other guy lost his footing once and acted politely surprised. Their anger progressed to frustration. Then Luc's opponent stepped back for a second, wound up and punched Luc in the jaw. Luc was incredulous. He shook his head slightly, and massaged the aching bone. 'I can't believe you hit me!' His opponent obviously couldn't believe it either, but the idea grew on him. He actually started to look pleased with himself. This made Luc very angry. He got his balance back, gathered his strength, and hit the guy so hard that he fell flat on the ground in a daze.

Kate was the first to speak. 'Who . . . What . . . Who was that?'

'My brother,' Luc answered calmly.

'He's your *brother* and you did that to him?'

'Yes. I introduce you.' He gestured toward his brother who was still lying on the ground in a heap. 'Antoine, Kate. Kate, Antoine. *D'accord*. Okay let's go.'

Kate trailed after him. 'What the hell is going on?'

They walked to the other side of the town and left the village on a dirt and gravel road that turned, first, into a wagon path through the forest, and then into a thin mountain trail. They walked for about twenty minutes without saying a single thing to each other. When they came to a crest in the hill, Luc slowed down and looked at the landscape that spread out in front of them. He took a deep breath, and an almost invisible trace of a smile came to his lips. They continued to walk.

'All this is Antoine's,' Luc started. 'This vineyard has been in the family for three generations. This is what we do, who we are. But as for Antoine, I don't know what he does. He is always so . . . sober.'

'And that's a bad thing, right?' Kate asked, only half sarcastic.

'Yes. Because he makes the wine, but he never drinks it, never enjoys it.'

'And, of course, you always drink it. So, why aren't you part of this? Why isn't half of it yours?'

Luc put on his evasive face. 'To make a great wine you have to take risks, you must have the soul of gambler.'

'So. You like to drink the wine and you like to gamble. We're getting close to an answer here, aren't we?'

'Yes,' he answered meekly. 'I gambled and I lost a lot. Sometimes I would even lose to Antoine. My dog. My first car . . .'

'He took your dog?'

'One night I was very drunk. You have to understand, I owed him a lot of money. He knew exactly what he was doing.' He spoke defensively.

'What was he doing?' Kate was still trying to process the part about the dog and couldn't keep up.

'I lost all of it to him. One hand of poker. Pouf.' He gestured lazily toward the vineyard.

Kate suddenly got the whole thing. 'You lost your birthright in a single hand of poker?'

'I'm an asshole. What can I tell you?' Luc laughed nervously and then went quiet again.

'And that's why you hate him. And he hates you.'

'*Oui*. That and . . . uh . . . well. That and I slept with his wife.' Luc was barely audible.

Kate was shocked. She went stiff, froze in her tracks. As she stood and watched Luc walk ahead, she felt like she was in a surreal soap opera. She couldn't believe Luc would actually sleep with his sister-in-law. Disconnected thoughts and reactions ran through her head – how could she hang out with this guy, get friendly with him, begin to get fond of him? Was something wrong with her judgement? She stopped for a moment to contemplate getting out of there, but realized that she had to stick with him. She still needed him.

'So, Luc, is that it for everyone? What about the rest of your family, your parents? Do you have other brothers and sisters that you speak to?'

'Nothing,' he answered flatly. 'It's over. It is all a bridge I burned. They . . . let's say, we have nothing to do with each other.'

'That's it? You're never going to try again?'

Luc threw his hands up, hopeless, and blew out some air. There was nothing left to do. The ties were severed, undone, kaput. His family hated him. They were all resigned to never seeing each other.

They walked on in silence, until their contemplation was interrupted by the sound of an approaching party. Footsteps, talking, laughter and then running and calling out. '*EH. LUC! C'EST TOI! Alors* . . .' First a distinguished old man came into view as they rounded a corner. Then some children, a few men and a woman, all with big warm smiles on their faces. All looked genuinely thrilled to see Luc.

Kate watched Luc try to keep his eyes to the ground but saw that he couldn't mask his happiness at seeing everyone again. After a moment's reluctance he suddenly shrugged and let a big smile come to his face as he raised his arms in anticipation of a huge family reunion. Following the patriarch's lead, everyone rushed toward him.

As Kate watched the scene between them, she knew she'd been duped by Luc again. This time, though, she understood that all his resistance and bluster about his family hating him had been a necessary hedge against sadness, that he had actually believed they hated him, or that he had to make himself think it so that he could create a life for himself.

Kate was swept up as everyone returned to the farmhouse. Without any noticeable effort, a giant table was set for lunch in the garden overlooking the valley. The sun shone as everyone slowly sipped their wine and as plates of pâté, stew and fresh salads circulated around the table. It was a charming, civilised, surprisingly genteel gathering, the kind of thing Kate dreamed of having for herself one day. She could hardly believe that someone from so perfect and simple a place could fashion himself into the grungy, pushy oaf she had met a few days before on the airplane.

As she ate her lunch and drank her wine she wondered why he was still trying to get into her bag. She let it go while Luc's father and sister gave her a long tour of the farm and then the winery.

Luc took her absence as an opportunity to rifle through her bag in search of the necklace. The feeling that his whole future depended upon finding it was only increased by being in such close proximity to the land he hoped to exchange it for. He loved it here. He could hardly let himself admit how much he had missed everything about it. He wanted to get back and start his vine grafts so badly he could literally taste his own desire. He approached Kate's knapsack with eager anticipation, but as he searched he became frantic. The necklace wasn't there.

'I'm fucked,' he cried. 'I'm fucked. It's all over. It's finished.' He felt all of the energy drain from his body. He dragged himself over to a garden bench and fell deep into a depressed trance. He no longer really cared if he lived, died, went on or not.

Kate found him there about forty-five minutes later. She didn't allow his obvious gloom to penetrate her feelings of happiness. She started teasingly: 'Fester, fester, fester. Rot, rot, rot. I am witnessing the process.' She feigned a look of concern before she looked around the valley that surrounded them. 'Poor you, you had to grow up here. Show me your room.'

They climbed a solid staircase up to a narrow hallway. Luc's room was at the end and off to the right. When he opened the door, it felt like they'd entered a time capsule. The country smell hit her first, then the golden filtered light. She noticed the perfectly ordered objects and books, the drawings, the models and a writing desk, so small and brittle it almost broke her heart. The walls were washed in a beautiful earthy colour that was impossible to obtain in the new world. Drawn to his bookshelf first, she looked at the old school notebooks, then ran her fingers over some small award statues and sculptures that he'd obviously made. The bed looked like it had been left ready for him to come home, any time. She watched Luc walk over to the window and put his fingers over a big, hand-carved wooden box resting beneath it. He lingered over it for a while, so she asked what it was.

'Oh, nothing. It's a project I did a long time ago.' His hand fell over the latch and he flipped it lazily, lost in thought. Underneath the lid was a cabinet full of small bottles and herb bundles, each inside its own exact compartment. It looked magical and medieval; like an artefact of a lost science.

'You made this? What is it for?' She searched his face for a clue to the side of him that had conceived of and produced this marvel, the side that she didn't know.

Luc took a deep breath. 'Okay, I will tell you. But first you must take some more wine. Go on.' He poured some into a glass and handed it to her. After she swallowed he asked her to describe the taste.

Kate felt embarrassed. She hated moments like this because she was sure that there was a right answer and that she couldn't find it. 'I don't know. It tastes kind of like a nice red wine.'

'I think you can do better than that.'

She put on her radio announcer's voice and said, 'A bold wine, with a hint of sophistication, yet rustic and lacking in pretension.' When she looked up he was staring at her blankly. She hurried to fill the gap of silence. 'I'm sorry, I was actually talking about myself. Luc, I don't know how to talk about wines.'

'But you're not wrong – wine is like people,' he reassured her. 'The grape takes in all of the

influences and the life around it, and absorbs them.
That's how it gets its personality.' He motioned to
the bottles in the box. 'Here in Provence there is
so much growing, all around the vineyards. Here,
smell this . . .' He carefully opened a small glass
bottle, the size of a perfume bottle, and put it under
her nose. Kate sniffed it and identified its contents:
rosemary. Luc opened another. He was impressed
when she recognised that it was dried mushroom.
'Very good,' he said. He went on opening bottles
and pinching little bundles of dried herbs. Kate
recognised them all: currant, lavender, cassis. Luc's
voice became more confident as he went along. 'All
of these are around here, in the ground and in the
air. The bees travel with them, the wind carries
them.' He held the glass to her lips again: 'Here,
taste the wine again.' When she took a small sip
and held it in her mouth Luc told her to close her
eyes.

Kate smiled in recognition. 'The currant, I
can taste that right away. And then the one
in the small brown bottle. Was it oak? And a
little lavender.' She took another sip and inhaled
slowly, savouring the taste and the feeling of little
pockets of wine slightly biting on different parts
of her tongue.

Luc watched her, as if he was studying her

face for the first time. It was like the moment in the train compartment. He almost reached out and touched her, but she opened her eyes and smiled, breaking the spell. 'That was incredible, really. And you made this box?'

'*Ah oui*, yes.' Luc spoke flatly. He suddenly remembered how depressed he was.

'Well, it's incredible,' Kate said. She loved his past and was thrilled at the respite it afforded from her string of horrors. She took another sip and gave Luc a peck on the cheek. 'Thanks. A lot.'

The tour of the house led to a discussion of Luc's dreams. And the discussion about his dreams led to a long walk to an abandoned vineyard on the other side of the mountain. Luc's father, Octave, walked a few steps behind them all of the way up the rugged hillside to a high plateau that overlooked the entire region. Directly beneath them stretched the land Luc had been lusting after. The vineyard was wild and dishevelled but it still had a magic to it. Off to one side was an old house that hadn't been lived in for years. Kate looked at it.

'Whose house is that?'

'No one comes here any more. The guy who had this place gave up a long time ago. But look,' he said as he dug up a handful of reddish dirt, 'the earth is good again. It's been resting. Some day I will buy this and I will make a great wine. Right here. The best in the region. On this wreck of a vineyard.'

As Kate watched him, she saw that his whole being was absorbed in this land. Everything his life had lost and everything that it wanted to be was resting dormant in this vineyard and his dream of what it could be. She interrupted his reverie. 'So, you would risk everything for this, wouldn't you?'

'*Oui*, of course.' Luc shrugged at the simplicity of the answer.

'You'd do anything to have it? You would get down on your knees and beg?' Luc looked at her curiously and nodded. Kate slowly sized him up and looked him in the eye before continuing. 'Then what makes you so different than me?' She waited for an answer, but none came. 'Admit it Luc, admit it, not much.'

Luc had nothing left to say. His eyes softened as he looked her squarely in the eye. 'Okay, I admit it. There.'

There was something awkward in the levelling that had just taken place. Kate nodded a little nervously. 'Okay . . . well . . . it really is beautiful here.'

Luc looked at her squarely for some time.

He realised that he ought to feel real gratitude towards Kate. She had actually helped bring him back, closer to himself. With nothing left to lose, he decided that he should help her. He should do everything that he could for her.

'I will help you get back Charlie,' he said suddenly. 'If you want him, we will get him back. Like I promised.'

There was about an hour of golden-white light left when they got back to the train station. Kate was feeling almost entirely better. Her detour in Provence had transformed all of her ideas about France, French culture and Luc, and she was actually starting to have fun. She'd never spent time so open-endedly, so aimlessly. Her happiness seemed to affect her view of everything – Luc was definitely looking much more human and interesting. He even seemed less sleazy out here in the country.

Kate listened to the train approaching in the distance and studied the landscape, bathed in the perfect Mediterranean light. She got up and sauntered mischievously over to Luc. The sound of the approaching train got louder. 'So tell me,' she began, 'how are you planning to buy that vineyard? You must have some kind of strategy, some long-term plan, no?'

Luc was concentrating on the train as it pulled into the station. '*Oui*, I had a plan. But it didn't work out.'

'What do you mean it didn't work out, what kind of plan was it?'

Luc was trying to keep this conversation brief. 'I had something to trade but, well . . .'

'What something?' Kate was being almost cruel in her persistence. 'You'll need some real money to buy that land. What was it? Bonds? Stocks? A little bag of plutonium?'

Luc wasn't in the mood. 'What does it matter, it didn't work out. That's all.'

'That's it? It just didn't work? If it was me, I'd have some kind of back-up plan. Something more than just bullshit and hot air to fall back on. Something maybe . . . like . . . *this!*' Kate yanked her shirt collar open and thrust out her neck to show him what she had hanging there. It was a strand of large cut diamonds set in white gold: beautiful, elegant and expensive. It was the necklace he'd been searching for. Kate closed her shirt before Luc could react and jumped on the train. She looked down at Luc, who stood on the platform in a daze, and inquired innocently, 'Coming?'

15

Luc was ecstatic. He decided that it wasn't malice on Kate's part, it was more sweet revenge, and a little liberation. For him it was the world. Everything returned to him, this time in better shape than before. His mind raced to restore all the perfect and fantastic images of his future which he had let slip away when he thought he'd lost the necklace. After a few delirious moments, though, he told himself to slow down and considered the matter immediately at hand: getting Charlie back for Kate. As they sat on the train, he began outlining the basic strategy.

'Okay, number one. Before going into the war, you must carefully choose the field of battle. You must have every advantage. Then you must be sure to really know your enemy; study him thoroughly.' As he spoke, they looked out toward the coastal towns. Perfectly planned and manicured public spaces, punctuated by majestic palm trees and designer-perfect people. 'You see,' he continued, 'with a woman like Juliette it is not just the looks that make her dangerous. It is the attitude.' Luc explained at great length how a woman like Juliette would have been trained, almost since birth, to be a complex and unreadable force. Then he moved on to lesson two. 'Americans, they have always put their cards on the table, right away. Like all your rot and fester bullshit. Forget it. You must learn to hold your cards close, and to play them one at a time.'

Kate couldn't resist teasing him about his own gambling skills, and about how these rules seemed to have failed him.

The train had come to a stop at the Cannes station and they were making their way through the crowds when she caught sight of a young couple sitting at a café table. The girl, sullen and beautiful, broke off from a passionate embrace with her boyfriend, turning away with a bored and slightly aggravated look on her face. Her lips curled and tightened. The boy tried to get her to speak, but she just shrugged dismissively. Kate had no name for this scenario, but she realised that she had seen it over and over again all over the country. Girls acting alternatively impassioned and detached, transfixed and put off. 'You see that?' she asked Luc. 'What's that – that pout? Juliette did that, I remember it perfectly.'

'This is one of the French woman's greatest weapons. Extraordinary, isn't it?'

'You mean the "I don't need you" routine works here?' Kate was trying to keep up.

'Yes. Because it is provocative. You see, these girls know how to say "yes" when they mean "no" and "no" when they mean "yes". The man is in a constant state of excitement and irritation.'

'A state he confuses with passion, I suppose.'

'Perhaps, but he is hooked. Do you understand?' Luc watched her roll her eyes, and took it as a yes. He smiled and continued: 'Okay, *très bien*. Now it is time for the armour, our costume. Come.'

Luc led the way through the streets towards the shopping district, where he surprised Kate

again. He behaved knowledgeably and confidently: shopping sprees apparently came easily to him.
They went to a few select stores and Luc displayed an unusual ability throughout to be tasteful,
encouraging and to have fun at the same time.
He suspended his lectures in French man-catching
techniques until they had left the last store and were
on their way to the hotel.

As they strolled along the Croisette, Luc gave
one final bit of advice. 'Now, remember, most
important. When Charlie sees you, he will be ready
for a scene. A drama. But don't give him the satisfaction. He will become immediately intrigued.
It is like not dropping the other shoe, as you call
it. Keep him wondering, waiting, even wanting
something more.'

Kate let it all soak in. She was amazed by the
level of glamour and sophistication sustained in
what was fundamentally a seaside resort. Men and
women were dressed and made-up, ready to have
dinner with the same people they had been lying,
practically naked, next to on the beach just hours
before. The jewellery was fantastic, too. And the
hair styles. Who had time to go to the hairdresser
on vacation?

As they approached the doors of the legendary
Carlton Hotel, Kate mentally prepared herself to

see Charlie and to be treated rudely by the staff.
Whatever came first.

They crossed the threshold and went through
the revolving door. Luc nodded to the doorman and whispered to Kate, 'Are you ready
for battle?' The question made Kate feel a little
more at ease, like she had a true accomplice
this time. They walked into a giant marble lobby. Everyone inside was dressed in co-ordinating
colours: coral, peach, almond, sienna. Their rings
and watches matched the chandeliers. It felt like
a conspiracy of style, working against her. Kate
began to explore the main floor and lobby, somewhat aimlessly, as Luc checked in at the front
desk.

The concierge read the card that Luc filled out.
'Monsieur Antoine Teyssier. And how will you
be paying?' Luc presented a credit card, stamped
with the name of his brother Antoine. There was
no problem. He selected a price and a room and
pocketed a set of keys. Having seen Kate disappear
toward the dining-room a few minutes before, he
wandered after her.

The lobby was the size of a small town square,
and just as active. Kate had made her way across
to where the restaurant entrances were. In a state
of complete fascination, she peeked into the café

and then took several steps into the main dining-room. It was like some stroke of awkward fate: within a second or two she realised that she was looking at Juliette and her family having dinner with Charlie. They were fifteen feet away, direct-ly in front of her. Her mind raced, but she felt as though her heart and body were moving in slow motion. She couldn't get over how distinguished they all looked, sitting there. All except Charlie, of course, who was even more ridiculously dressed than the last time, in a loud Italian designer floral shirt and a navy linen jacket. His hair looked like a single congealed mass, like a guy in a sports car ad. She fully expected to look down and see him sockless in fine leather loafers. He was listening to Juliette's overly handsome father with a look of rapt interest on his face – false, if she had to guess. His eyes momentarily glanced in Kate's direction. He didn't seem to see her, but he flinched slightly and lost his concentration. His eyes darted anx-iously around the room, as Kate ducked behind a large planter. She peeked out for another look at the *haute bourgeoise* family.

Juliette had noticed Charlie was distracted and spoke disapprovingly. 'Charlie, is everything okay?'

'Um. No. Well . . . I think I just saw Kate.'

Juliette tried to calm his fears. 'I'm sure it's just your imagination. Now, please . . .' She smiled politely at her parents. But this only brought the rest of them into the disturbance, and they all politely stopped eating until Charlie's problems were smoothed out.

Kate scuttled sideways again, behind a large plant. There was no way she wanted to be spotted in this situation. In an attempt to ensure that she was completely hidden, she took another step back, her eyes fixed on Charlie. As she did so, something caught her leg. Losing her balance, she went flying backwards over the three-tiered dessert trolley standing behind her. She tipped over all the cakes, tarts and custards as she went, landing in a gooey heap on the floor, face first in a mound of cream and sponge. Several silver trays came crashing to the marble floor after her.

The sound echoed through the elegant restaurant. Charlie jumped to his feet in a kind of panicked trance: every instinct told him that Kate was lurking around there somewhere.

'I'll be right back, I've got to go check something out,' he mumbled nervously. He walked out towards the mess, intent on clearing up the mystery – and deeply anxious about its outcome.

Juliette tsk-ed and huffed out after him, thoroughly put off by his neurotic behaviour. 'Kate is not here. Now come and sit down, my parents are beginning to wonder. Come on, Charlie.' But Charlie had to be sure. Shrugging Juliette off, he demanded of first a waiter, then a bellhop if they had seen a blonde woman in a white shirt. Both responded with the same exasperated tone. Yes, she came through here and went that way. Charlie set off in pursuit.

Luc was searching for Kate as well. He spotted her first, and his jaw dropped when he saw her. Crawling on hands and knees across the marble floor towards the elevators, she was completely covered in cake and icing, leaving a trail of slime behind her. Just as she disappeared from view behind a pillar, Charlie arrived from the other direction. He glanced at Luc and then beyond him, still searching. Luc recognised him instantly from the little photograph in Kate's locket. He felt a surge of aggression that only half surprised him. Charlie was a privileged boy in training for a comfortable and cushioned manhood. He took all of his good fortune for granted and dressed like a wimp.

Luc watched as Juliette came out again, subdued Charlie and led him back to her parents. He was deeply impressed that a jerk like Charlie could handle as beautiful and formidable a girlfriend as Juliette.

Kate and Luc found each other in the elevator lobby. Without speaking or even admitting that they knew each other, they made their way up to their room, a large one-bedroom suite on the fifth floor overlooking the Mediterranean sea. The room was as luxurious as any Kate had ever seen. Large sofas and armchairs, a gilded desk in front of wide french doors that opened on to the turquoise sea. She felt distinctly out of place.

Going into the bathroom, she began to pick the cake and cream out of her hair and clothes. She didn't know what to say. Luc stayed in the bedroom pacing furiously as he silently composed his tirade. When he couldn't stand it any more, he started to rant through the bathroom door.

'You really don't understand a word I tell you. How can I help you win back this ridiculous man if you act like a clown?'

'It was an accident, okay?' Kate couldn't believe that Luc thought she had intended to find Charlie and humiliate herself again. 'I wasn't expecting to see him right then. With her family. Sucking up to her father. And did you see her, her skimpy dress, the way she was cutting her food into tiny little chewable pieces?'

'*Oui*, I saw her. She was . . . kind of . . .' Luc said, his eyes lighting up.

'What,' Kate snapped. 'What was she?'

Luc loved having something to wind her up about again. 'Well she was . . . mmm . . . definitely a . . .' He let his eyes roll up a bit to suggest that he was conjuring up a pleasing image.

'I know what you're saying. That I'm not sexy enough, right?'

'I did not say anything at all.' He feigned a complete lack of malice.

'But,' Kate went on, 'that's what you want me to be. Some ridiculous pouty little girl who says "yes" when she means "no" and "no" when she means "yes".'

'No I do not.' Luc shrugged her off.

'No? Meaning what, Luc? Yes or no? The whole thing is ridiculous. Happy – smile.' She grimaced. 'Sad, frown. I use a corresponding face for an emotion. But no, what you want is some sexy and sadistic mystery bimbo.'

'*Non*. It's not me who wants anything. I don't want it.'

'Then what *do* you want?'

Luc became suddenly quiet and thoughtful.

He took her hand in his, in an attempt to make his point sincerely. 'I want you . . .' he said, the words coming out with the wrong emphasis.

Kate looked at him in shock. 'You want me . . . ?'

'I want you . . . to make Charlie suffer. To be tempted and intrigued. I want you . . . to make him feel that even though you are standing right in front of him that you are gone. That he can't have you. Okay? Well, that's all.' He drew back and let her hand drop away.

It was late. Their exchange had left them both feeling jangled and unsure about their next move. In an effort to escape the tension and uncertainty, Kate retreated to the shower. She stayed under the warm water for a long time; she had to wash her hair three times to get the crumbs and grease out.

Standing under the hot stream of water, she realised that she was procrastinating. She didn't want to get out of the shower, because it was a good place to stop and reflect. Everything was moving towards Charlie at an accelerated rate, and she had a strange sensation that her desire for him was being altered or interrupted by her adventure. She was also afraid of sleeping in the same room as Luc, but she couldn't believe she was even acknowledging such ideas. She stayed in the shower as long as she could before drying off and putting on a huge, white T-shirt. Then she quickly opened the bathroom door, went straight for the queen-size bed, and tucked herself in. When she turned out her light the room was almost dark. Luc turned away from her and undressed beside the formal looking sofa he was going to sleep on. Kate couldn't help watching him. She tried to assure herself that it was friendly curiosity. But he looked very good in silhouette. They remained silent until he lay down on the couch and covered himself in a woollen blanket.

'Luc?' Kate spoke softly as she stared at the ceiling.

'*Oui?*' Luc perked up at the attempt at communication.

'Do you . . .'

'*Oui* . . .' He wasn't even sure what he wanted her to say.

Everything hung in the air for a moment. Both their minds raced and their hearts slowed. 'Do you think I have a chance? With Charlie, I mean. After what happened in the restaurant?'

'Yes', he said finally, 'and tomorrow we will turn your mistake to our advantage.' That was it. Neither of them spoke again until the next day.

16

THEY PLANNED ALL THE DAY'S MOVEMENTS FROM the moment they woke up. Kate put on new clothes, a simple French fisherman's sweater and trousers, in an effort to appear perfectly relaxed and at home. They sat in an outdoor café for a while and planned and argued and plotted.

After breakfast they followed Charlie and Juliette to the fancy beach club. Luc gave Kate one last talking to as they watched them descend the steps to their spot on the beach. 'You see, Charlie is still wondering if he saw you. You are now like a ghost, a phantom. Your memory will infect them, their rapport. That's very good. Do you see how his field of vision has completely opened up. He suspects everything. You are lurking in every wide-open space.'

They watched Charlie and Juliette undress and get settled. 'Now, just when they are starting to look comfortable again, you will strike.' They waited another ten minutes before moving over to the club's entrance.

Kate found it easy to prepare herself. It was a great game now. And like all good games of your own creation, it was going to be very hard to lose. She walked confidently over to where Charlie and Juliette were lying on the beach and poked her head between them. 'Hey stranger,' she said with a big smile, her face inches away from Charlie's.

Charlie choked on his Orangina. 'Kate?' he sputtered. He leaned forward, swung round and sat looking at her with his mouth hanging half open.

'I came all this way,' Kate said warmly. 'Aren't you two even going to offer me a seat?'

Juliette spoke English with the accent of a haughty Parisian who has learned it at a British boarding school. She looked as if none of this had fazed her, as if nothing that Kate was capable of ever would. 'But of course, please have a seat,' she said, cocking her head gently to one side.

Kate pulled a *chaise* from another aisle and rolled it around to face away from the sun. She sat down, facing the two of them. At first she completely ignored Charlie and addressed Juliette with a big phoney smile. 'So,' she said, 'you must be Charlie's Juliette.' Juliette nodded confidently. Kate went on. 'Let me take a look at the woman who stole my Charlie's little heart.'

Juliette stiffened her spine and raised her chin before coolly replying, 'I did not steal anything that didn't want to be stolen.'

Kate threw an impressed grin towards Charlie. 'Ooh. Ouch. That was pretty good. She might be smart, Charlie. And she's definitely beautiful. Probably great . . .' – Kate paused to think for a moment – '. . . at everything.'

Charlie couldn't stand it any longer. Not only wasn't Kate supposed to be here, she wasn't supposed to be acting so strangely and powerfully when she did get here. He got up nervously and tried to speak. 'Look, Kate. Please . . .'

Kate took command of the situation. 'Charlie, quiet.' Charlie stopped talking and looked to her for whatever was going to happen next. 'Sit.' She signalled to emphasise her direction. Charlie fell into his chair obediently. 'Look, guys,' Kate went on, 'believe it or not, I didn't come here for a fight.' A waiter walking past caught her attention. 'Excuse me. Waiter. Hi. I don't speak much French, so bear with me. I'd like a sea breeze. Does that translate?' He nodded, yes. Kate grinned condescendingly and turned back to Charlie and Juliette. 'The key to French waiters? If you're nice to them, they'll treat you like shit. However, if you treat them like shit, they love you.' She leaned over and plucked a stick of celery from Juliette's vegetable basket. 'Mind?' She started to munch on it, and realised that Charlie and Juliette were staring at her, dumbfounded. 'What? What is it, Charlie?'

'Nothing. It's just, I mean, you seem so different.' Charlie was saying it half as an explanation to Juliette.

'Yeah. I'm going through some sort of transition thing. I hope it's not hysteria. You see, after you called me, I decided to get on a plane to Paris and get you back.' She turned directly to Juliette. 'And I hate to fly. In fact, I never fly. Isn't that right, Charlie? But I told myself there was no way that everything I had been building towards

would be destroyed because some pouting little –
and this is before I knew you personally – ' she
flashed a sweet smile at Juliette, 'bitch, pardon
my French, wanted to steal herself a husband. I
bought the ticket, got on the plane and somehow
made it over the big blue ocean.' She stopped for
a moment, as if to denote that a new chapter was
about to start. 'And then, the most extraordinary
thing happened.'

Juliette looked to Charlie. Charlie looked to
Kate. 'What happened?' he asked.

'Everything that could possibly go wrong, went
wrong. I was wandering the streets of Paris, pen-
niless and without a hope in the world. Well, let
me tell you, you can do a lot of soul-searching at
a moment like that. I even searched your soul,
Charlie. And I realised that I had spent my entire
adult life trying to protect myself against exactly
this kind of situation. So much of what I did was
in the name of prevention. But, guess what? You
can't do it. There's no home safe enough, no relationship secure enough, no country nice enough.
You're just setting yourself up for a bigger fall
and having a really boring time in the process.'
She paused again, for effect, and looked over to
the entrance way. 'That's when I took up with
Luc.'

'Who is Luke?' asked Charlie dully.

Just as Kate began to correct Charlie's pronunciation she caught sight of Luc making his way through the rows of sunbathers. She waved to him. 'Luc! Over here.'

Luc swaggered up, smiled at everyone and pretended to assess the situation and figure it all out. He mumbled to Kate in French. And then he backed away, as if to let them work out their business in peace.

'Who is he? What did he say?' Charlie was flabbergasted – and extremely curious.

'I dunno. I think it was something about you guys. Luc doesn't speak much English, but we seem to manage just fine.' Kate looked all relaxed and happy to see Luc.

'You do?' Charlie was not getting any of it.

'Yeah. Maybe it's just the transitional thing, you know, to help me to get over us. I mean, that's probably what's going on. But . . . what the hell.' She threw up her hands, smiling. 'I'm here.'

'What does Luc do?' Charlie whispered.

Kate frowned, a little perplexed but not bothered. 'You know, besides what we do together, I don't think he does anything at all.' She looked back over to Luc and saw him signal with his watch that it was time to get going. Getting up, she shook hands with Juliette before she addressed Charlie in a friendly, but business-like tone. 'Let's have dinner tonight, and go over who does what and who keeps what. We can clear it all up before I go home.'

Baffled and intrigued by everything that was going on, Charlie accepted immediately, without even looking to Juliette for a sign of support.

Kate calmly walked off with Luc towards the boardwalk, leaving Charlie and his new fiancée to deal with her bombshell. She managed to control herself until she was sure they couldn't see her any more. Then she burst out, 'I loved that. It was amazing. I felt . . . I don't know . . . released.'

Luc congratulated her unconditionally. 'You were fantastic, incredible. You were made for this country! They were completely destroyed. It's perfect. You will meet him tonight for dinner, and concentrate on the details of your split up. Go for the minutiae. It will gnaw at him. By morning you will be queen of the castle again, I promise you. Now, we must celebrate. Some wine, *non*, champagne! Wait, I will be back in two minutes with some champagne.' Luc left Kate in a small park and hurried off towards the shopping streets north of them.

Kate was quietly exhilarated. She sat down on a bench overlooking the sea. She hadn't felt so high in years, and for the first time since her trip began she realised that she was very happy not to be at home. France was beautiful, liveable and exciting. She watched the people come and go through the little park.

Suddenly she heard her name. 'Kate.' The deep French voice was charming and seductive. In the swirl of the moment she wondered if it was the voice of a narrator of a forties movie. 'Kate, I would like to talk with you for a moment, may I?'

'I'm sorry, do we know each other?' she said politely to the tall, slightly familiar gentleman standing by the bench. He produced a police badge and sat himself down next to her. '*Non*, but we have a mutual acquaintance, Luc Teyssier.' Although Kate did not immediately recognise the man, she was sure she had seen him before. 'He's actually much more of a friend than an acquaintance,' mused Jean-Paul. 'That is why I've come to talk to you. About a necklace.'

Kate went into dipstick routine. 'Oh, the necklace. His dead aunt gave it to him. He didn't declare it, I know. What kind of penalty will he have to pay to keep it?' She kept a co-operative grin on her face as long as she could sustain it. The detective just stared at her, deeply and honestly. He could have waited all day. 'So,' Kate finally said, 'if he stole it, why don't you just arrest him?'

Jean-Paul spoke firmly and deliberately. 'I'm old-fashioned. I owe him a large debt, much bigger than a debt of money.' He sounded wise and loyal. 'So I ask you to talk to him. The necklace can be returned, anonymously, to me, tomorrow. That's all I want.'

'He'll never agree. He can't.'

'He must,' he said emphatically. Getting up, he handed her a paper with his local phone number on it. He started to walk off, then turned to add, 'No one in Cannes will buy the necklace. I have made sure of that.'

When Luc returned with the champagne, Kate stepped right back into the mood that he had left her in. The detective's request was too hard and too impossible to consider now. They enjoyed their wine, every last drop, as they watched the sunset, and then meandered back to the hotel to get ready for Kate's big dinner with Charlie. As they passed Cartier's, Luc boldly announced that he would come there first thing in the morning and sell the necklace. Tomorrow was the day.

Suddenly, in its entirety, a brilliant plan presented itself to Kate. She wondered if it was the champagne that oiled the wheels. 'Luc, why don't I sell the necklace?'

'You? What do you mean? Why?' Luc said.

'Well, because, um, well if I can quote you – because I am me and you are you. And if *I* go into Cartier's, you know . . .'

'Yes.' Luc was catching on. 'You go in dressed nicely, *toute propre*, smiling your little smile, walking your little walk, playing the foreigner, the widow, whatever. You're right, you'll do much better than me.' By the time they reached the Carlton lobby, their plan was made, her wardrobe was chosen and the scenario was completely mapped out. And by the time they were in the elevator to their room, they were both wondering what would happen tonight.

17

WHILE KATE DRESSED IN THE BATHROOM, LUC WAS goind through a remarkable transformation of his own. With his hair clean and his face closely shaven, his cool blue eyes lost their sleazy sheen and were truly sexy. He also put on the first light-coloured and well designed clothes that Kate had ever seen him in: a silk collarless dress shirt with a beige linen waistcoat and matching trousers, generously cut and elegant. Even his posture improved in fine clothes. When he had checked himself out in the mirror for the last time, Luc went over to his leather jacket and pulled out the diamond necklace. He held it in his hand for a moment and then carefully slipped it into his vest, like an old-fashioned pocket-watch. He tuned the radio to some pleasant music, mixed a batch of Martinis at the mini-bar, then sat down on the bed with his feet up, and stared off at the dark sea.

Kate was dressed and ready quickly but stayed in the bathroom for a long time. First she stared at the telephone number that the detective gave her, then she stared at herself in the mirror and went over her options. Finally she made the call. She arranged everything for the next morning. When she hung up she heard Luc calling to her asking her if she wanted a drink. 'Sure, I'll just be a second,' she answered.

She opened the door and stood in the door-way for a long time, afraid to enter the room in her new cocktail dress. It was icy blue, almost white, had spaghetti straps and hugged her body all the way to the tops of her legs. Then it flared gently and lightly. Short and sexy, it suited her perfectly.

To break the tension, she smiled and said, 'I bought it at the store downstairs. Like it?'

Luc sat up, put his feet back on the ground and reached for a Martini to hand her. 'You look wonderful. Was it expensive?'

She nodded meekly. He continued, 'You charged it to the room?' She nodded, more tentatively this time. 'Great!' Luc exclaimed. 'No problem.' Then he reached into his pocket and pulled out the necklace.

'Wear this tonight, it's perfect for you.'

Kate blanched. 'I don't think that's such a good idea, Luc.'

'I insist. It will be your charm, your good luck charm.' He reached behind her neck and fastened it on her. 'Who is the *goddesse* now?' He gestured grandly and theatrically, inviting her to dance. She responded in kind. They danced smoothly and close. Luc leaned into her and spoke softly. 'Now, you must remember. You don't need him. Make him work, make him sweat. It's killing him that you are over him so easily, so quickly . . . You are over him, aren't you?' He raised his eyebrows teasingly.

'Stop it, Luc.' Kate thought for a moment and added, 'What did you think of him?'

'He's not so bad in person. Still, that chin, so weak, it makes me wonder. And his ridiculous wardrobe.' Luc pulled back and looked at Kate for a moment. They each took a sip of their Martinis and went on with their dance. 'Do you know what I'm going to do for you tonight?' Luc asked. 'To ensure your victory.'

'What?' Kate listened warily.

'Ju-li-ett-e.'

'Juliette?' Kate was forestalling having to deal with what he was suggesting.

Luc continued to dance and talk. 'She will be a little sad tonight, a little angry. A little, um, vulnerable. It is a word? So I will find her and I will . . . um . . . comfort her.'

So this was why he was all dressed up. Kate couldn't believe it. Guys would use any opportunity, wouldn't they? She tried to contain her cynicism, but only managed to moderate it. 'I wouldn't want you to do anything too unpleasant, Luc.'

She didn't feel it, but Luc sank a bit. The whole situation had taken on a life of its own. And neither of them felt the conviction they once had. Kate decided to lighten things up again. After all, what did she care who he slept with. 'But what about your little, you know, your little . . . ?'

'*Oui*. My little problem. Well, I feel like tonight my problem won't be a problem. I feel suddenly, like you – relaxed. And even if it is a problem, it won't be about my pleasure, it will be about hers. You don't disapprove of that do you? I will find her and I will – '

'Luc,' she interrupted, 'ssh, let's just dance, okay?' So they danced until the song ended, each thinking about the evening ahead. Then they silently drank their Martinis, using the distraction of the perfect ocean view to prevent them from having to deal with each other any more. At eight-thirty Kate left to see Charlie for dinner.

18

KATE MET CHARLIE AT ONE OF THE MOST ELEGANT
and expensive restaurants in Cannes. They walked
over to their table on pale, intricately woven
carpets. The Maître'd pulled out a soft and
thickly upholstered armchair for Kate to sit in,
and motioned to a waiter to bring them drinks
immediately. Kate was glad she had dressed up.
She blended, for the first time since the grungy
café back in Paris. Charlie had another new and
ridiculous outfit on. But his hair and face looked
better than ever. The Riviera sun was doing the job
it was paid to do. He was the sexiest-looking man in

the room. After they were seated and had ordered drinks, Kate slipped a thin pad of paper and a pen out of her evening bag. She looked up to Charlie, smiled a big friendly smile and began.

'Okay, so I've been going over a few things in my mind. Obviously, I keep the condo. You'll be able to afford much better when your practice gets bigger. And we'll each keep everything that we came into the relationship with. Right? So we've just got to deal with the stuff we both love, or bought together. I keep the bonsai, and the black lamp we got is yours. Next is the love-seat in the living-room.' She lifted her eyes from the list and looked at him sincerely. 'Tell me if you think this is crazy, but how about we get a chainsaw, cut it in half and make two chairs? That should do the trick, shouldn't it?'

Charlie couldn't stand it. 'Can we not talk about this? It's too depressing, isn't it?'

'It's business, Charlie.' She was using her warmest and most understanding teacher's voice. 'It's the business of breaking up. If you can't handle it, why don't I just have a yard sale and send you half the money?' She was secretly overjoyed: he was responding perfectly.

His chest was tightening. 'You just hate me, don't you?'

Kate pondered for a second, then shook her head decisively. 'Actually, I don't. Now, the CDs. They'll be tough. Why don't I just keep them all?'

'You don't hate me?' Charlie had to crack her armour. It was killing him. She just shrugged like she didn't know what he was talking about. His heart began to ache. He suddenly missed her. Missed her love. He felt like a lost fool on his way down.

'Sweetie?' Kate moved in close to study him. 'Are you crying? Your eyes look all moist and weird.'

Charlie braced himself and tried to think of something else. 'No! I was just feeling so guilty. So stupid and guilty.'

Kate sat back her seat, looking relaxed and a little indifferent. 'Well, I'm not going to tell you not to feel guilty. Not any more. In fact, I think you should swim in it, feel as guilty as you want.'

Charlie laughed incredulously. 'You're amazing, you really are,' he said, then glanced around the room. 'Will you dance with me? A last dance. Please?' He reached across the table, gently took her hand in his.

He walked with her to the dance floor. A

three-piece band was playing in the corner. They danced like they used to. Charlie was soon close to her, much faster than Kate was ready for. He let his cheek fall next to hers. 'You seem so different,' he said softly. 'Or is it more of the same? It's like there's a light on inside of you now, illuminating all of the best parts. Who turned it on? Why wasn't it me?' With his head so close now, he couldn't resist brushing his lips against her neck and kissing her. Within a moment they were kissing deeply and passionately.

Kate tried to appear totally and passionately responsive while she unravelled the swirl of contradictory emotions inside her. She had Charlie back in her arms, and the relief was making her light-headed. But, on the other hand, she had Charlie back in her arms and she felt like she needed a protective coating on so she could test out how she felt about it. After a few moments' hesitation she let herself go. She blocked out everything but the most romantic and positive of feelings.

Within a short time they were on their way back to the hotel. Arriving at the room, they stumbled, grabbed and kissed their way over to the bed and fell on to it, already abandoned to the idea of the full reinstatement of their couplehood.

'Please forgive me, please forgive me, I must have been insane,' Charlie repeated over and over again between kisses.

Kate couldn't think of anything to say back to him. As he kissed her she wondered why. Did she agree with him about being insane? Was she being bitchy and letting him grovel for a while longer? Was it possible that the apology meant more than the reunion? Did she want him or did she want to win? She went over the whole evening in her head. Charlie, meanwhile, was getting into the love-making. His clothes were coming off, he had moved on top of her. She heard him moaning, 'Kate, oh Kate'. She realised that she was doing an out-of-body thing. She was watching herself get Charlie back, without enjoying a single moment of it. She heard herself talking. 'Stop. *Stop, Charlie, now.*' She yanked his hair, hard.

Charlie was dazed and a little drunk. 'Ow, darling . . . what . . . ?'

Kate turned on him. 'Charlie, why wasn't it you who turned on the light, that big shining light that burns so bright now that you just can't resist dumping your new fiancée for your old one?'

'What?'

'Who are you, Charlie? Do you have any idea what you want?'

'You, I want you,' he said, sounding convinced.

'Well, twelve hours ago all you wanted was Juliette.' Kate stared him down and waited for him to justify himself. She was sitting up now and slowly inching herself backward, towards the foot of the bed.

'I know, I know, but . . .' Charlie tried to rise to the occasion. He sat up tall and faced her. He leaned into her as he spoke. 'Juliette is wonderful, she's exciting, and when I met her I wasn't thinking. You know how sometimes you just do things, you don't think about them? You just need to do them, do what you are feeling. But obviously, I was wrong. Or maybe I wasn't wrong. Maybe I was so afraid about having to buy that house, afraid of . . .'

'Getting married?' Kate asked.

'Yes.' Charlie looked her straight in the eye when he answered her.

'But you're not afraid of getting married to her.' Kate saw him struggling to come up with an answer. She went on. 'Since the telephone call, when you told me about her, I've been asking myself: What did I do wrong? What did I do?

Was I too controlling? Maybe, but that would make you a wimp. Was I not supportive enough? It wasn't that. Maybe I didn't have enough sexy underwear. But you could have bought it for me.'

Charlie thought of something to say. 'I will, I will . . .'

'Uh, uh. I don't want it. Because no matter what I might look like tonight, it's the same me from yesterday you'd wind up with tomorrow. The same old me who wants the house and family, who wants to . . . I don't know . . . plant some roots and see them grow.'

'You want to be a farmer?' he asked, then immediately regretted it. 'I'm sorry.'

'There is just one thing I don't want any more,' she said quietly.

There was a pause.

'Me?' Charlie asked tentatively.

'You. Sorry, Charlie.'

She decided to get out of there, and quickly left the room. She didn't know where to go and had no idea what Luc might be up to. The thought of it depressed her so much she took off and went for a long walk through the old part of town.

Luc was certainly up to something. Shortly after Kate left to meet Charlie, he took a tour of the neighbouring bars and cafés, hunting for Juliette. He was sure he'd find her and he was right. He recognised her from the back when he went into a small dark bar at one of the expensive hotels. She was wearing a pale-blue dress with a completely scooped-out back. Her hair was loose and fell past her shoulder-blades. It was thick and gorgeous. She was smoking sombrely and drinking a glass of red wine.

Juliette let him sit down with her and order a drink. She thought that at the very least he'd be a good enough whipping-boy to spend the evening with. It had only been about an hour since Charlie had gone to meet Kate, and it felt like for ever. She was pleased to find out how much Luc understood about her Charlie.

'You're right.' Juliette was in full flow in no time, getting more and more animated. 'There is something about his chin. Sometimes it makes me feel like hitting him.'

'You are wasted on him, really,' Luc told her.

'No,' Juliette said, retreating a bit. 'He's wonderful. And he tried so hard to make me laugh. He tells the silliest jokes. Stupid jokes. When I finally laugh, his face is lit up like a little boy's. So sweet. Not like a French man, not like . . . Well, you know.' She paused again. It was clear that she was thinking of Charlie and Kate. 'How could he agree to see her, how could he . . . ?' She fell deeper into depression. 'A year ago this would never have happened. I would have him in the bedroom while she waited all night for him to show up . . .' She touched his arm, and cupped her hands in his. 'Look at me. And tell me what you see.'

Luc smiled warmly. He knew that from now on, the evening was his. He ordered them each another drink and moved in close to answer her question, well aware of how to foster the right mixture of revenge and romance in Juliette. Before they drained their glasses they too were on their way back to the hotel. They probably hit the bed at the exact time as Kate and Charlie. They were in a frenzy. There was something sickly exciting for Luc about seducing Charlie's other girlfriend, especially as Juliette was so beautiful. Some kind of conquest by proxy. Most important of all, though, it was working! His problem wasn't a problem. They embraced tightly and tumbled onto the bed. As they rolled over, Luc heard her speaking to him. She was quietly calling his name, over and over again.

'Luc . . . Luc . . . Oh . . .'

'Kate, *oui* . . .'

And then he stopped. Shit. It was like a lightning bolt had hit him. 'What did I just say?'

'What *did* you just say?' Juliette was indignant. She pulled herself off him. She watched him as he lay on the bed in a stupor, confused and self-absorbed. There was nothing to say. So she poured a vase of water over him, collected her handbag and sweater, and walked out.

Luc couldn't sleep, he couldn't drink, he didn't want to watch TV or talk to anyone. He didn't want to have to deal with what he had just found out about himself. Or with her problems. He took a walk, just like Kate's, through the old city. They each walked for hours, but didn't run into each other. At about four o'clock, Kate went back to the room and Luc sat down in a beautiful square that overlooked the whole town. He sat looking out towards the harbour until the sun was up and the streets were busy again.

19

Luc knocked at the door tentatively and waited for the answer. When he heard a 'Come in, it's open', he stepped inside and said good morning. He looked around the room quickly for clues about what might have happened the night before, but didn't see any. 'So. How did it go? What happened to the lucky guy?'

Kate was curled up in an armchair eating a croissant and sipping a coffee. She studied him carefully before answering. She noticed a smear of lipstick on his shirt and tensed up a little bit. 'He wants to come back. On his hands and knees.'

Luc looked her in the eye. '*Très bien*. Congratulations.'

Kate tried to lighten up. 'So. It doesn't look like you had any problems. The old bull is back in business?' He shrugged modestly.

'Well,' Kate continued, 'let's get going and unload this necklace.'

They dressed silently and left the hotel. It was only minutes to the Cartier store. Luc nervously gave Kate instructions, repeating himself several times, and then moved across the street to wait for the outcome.

Once inside the store, Kate moved to the back where she had arranged to meet Jean-Paul. 'Bonjour,' she said faint-heartedly.

'Bonjour, mademoiselle. Thank you for coming.' They sat down. 'Now, *bon*,' said Jean-Paul, getting down to business, 'everything is as you said.' He reached into his breast-pocket. 'The . . . egg?'

'Nest egg,' corrected Kate.

'*Oui*, it was wired from your bank in Toronto this morning. Cartier's has agreed to issue this cheque' – he drew it out of his pocket – 'for the exact amount, in exchange. The illusion is complete.' He handed her the cheque, then watched as she took the necklace out of her pocket and handed it to him.

'Thank you,' Kate said. She looked down at the cheque for a long time. Then she carefully folded it into thirds and placed it in the pocket where the necklace had been.

Jean-Paul looked at her hard, but spoke softly. 'Why are you doing this? You are not with Luc, you'll probably never see him again.'

'Probably not,' Kate replied bluntly. 'Maybe it's payment in kind, for what he gave me. Or maybe it's just a . . . way of starting fresh. Does that make any sense?'

Jean-Paul nodded politely. 'I must come to Canada some day. You are a very sympathetic people, I think.'

'Oh, I'm not really a Canadian,' Kate replied. 'In fact I am currently "stateless".' She looked down at the necklace resting on the table. 'Just out of curiosity, how much is it really worth?'

'Over one hundred thousand dollars,' Jean-Paul said gravely.

Kate shook her head and got up from the little jeweller's table. She and the detective exchanged goodbyes and she left to find Luc across the street.

When she reached him, he was worn out from pacing. She showed him the cheque and he threw a fit. 'Sixty-two thousand dollars! *C'est pas possible.* What did you tell them? Why did I listen to you and your little walk and . . . Shit . . .' He looked to the heavens and mumbled in French, 'Why are you doing this to me now?'

Kate nervously grabbed his arm and started to speak. 'He said there was a flaw. Two of the big stones had these flaws. He said that they were beautiful diamonds, but officially, these flaws . . . I'm sorry, Luc.'

Luc calmed down. He lifted his head suddenly and addressed her again with a new attitude. 'It's going to be fine.'

'What?'

'It'll work out. The money. It will be just enough to get the land, right? Okay, so it won't be enough to get all the vines right away, or to do the transplanting and grafting . . . but in time. In time.' He started to walk down the boardwalk, engrossed in his thoughts, plotting and planning. 'I'll have to work at one of the other vineyards part-time for a while. Then I'll get my father back into it. Did you see how excited he was about the land? It'll take longer, maybe even five or six years before we get a decent bottle of wine . . .' Everything was going to be okay. He stopped racing, turned towards her and gently kissed her on the forehead. 'Thank you, thank you very much. You are my angel of luck. Who would have thought it.'

Standing close together, they looked at each other, but neither of them could find the words or the courage to say what they wanted to say. Finally Kate gracefully reached up and kissed him on each cheek, French style. It was a goodbye kiss. She stepped back and shrugged her shoulders. 'I've gotta go. Charlie is waiting for me.'

Luc didn't do a thing to dissuade her. He stepped back, bowed his head a bit and kept walking backwards, slowly. 'Goodbye Kate. Good luck, eh?' He watched her walk off for a moment or two, and then turned and walked away in the opposite direction. He decided to keep clear of the hotel until he was sure he wouldn't run into Charlie and Kate having their reunion. Stopping at a beachside café, he ordered himself a big, distracting meal.

From Luc's vantage point at the café, he could see at least a quarter of a mile along the curving coastline, and he looked up often while he was eating to watch the tourists. While he was finishing his omelette, he was sure he could see Juliette coming toward him. She was a long way off, and she was with somebody. As they came closer into view, he realised that it was Charlie.

He was scampering after her, obviously begging her forgiveness. And she was playing hard to get.

Luc couldn't believe it. He kept on eating, seemingly unaffected, as though it were a TV drama. So Kate lied to him. It had been a clean goodbye. An American goodbye. Fine. He figured that she had probably left the hotel already. He continued to eat methodically, watching Charlie and Juliette, who were now embracing. They began to kiss each other passionately. As his mind raced to gloss over his loss, he heard a familiar voice behind him.

'Ah. True love is wonderful, isn't it, my friend?'

Luc turned and found the ubiquitous Jean-Paul standing behind him. 'What are you doing here?' he said.

Jean-Paul sat down before he answered. 'Some jerk used a stolen credit card to pay his hotel bill. I've taken care of it, though.'

Luc returned his attention to the lovers, now walking hand in hand. 'Anyway, that's not true love.'

'Maybe, maybe not. You can't know for sure. But I know of another one, a true one, a wonderful one. Do you want to hear it?'

Luc was barely paying attention to him. He sounded like he couldn't care less. 'Does it have a happy ending?'

'I'm not sure yet. For that I need help — maybe you can help.' He pulled Luc's plate and newspaper away from him and moved his chair in closer before he began to talk again.

Kate sat back in her seat and gripped the armrests. She had decided to take her chances with Canadian immigration and try and charm her way back in. She was as anxious as ever about the flight, though. And this plane was very small compared with the one she'd taken to Paris from Toronto. She listened to the monotone voice over the loudspeaker, did her breathing and relaxation exercises, and started to hum her stupid song. She finally closed her eyes and conjured up her images of a stone cottage, this time in Provence, rolling hills planted with rows of grapevines and the incredible beauty of the yellow light that hung in the air, over it all. This image was working. She knew she could fly.

She kept her eyes closed and felt the doors of the plane shut. Before the plane began to roll away from the gate she felt someone sit down next to her. She kept her eyes closed, wanting to hold her concentration. Then she heard the voice.

'Kate . . .'

'Yes . . .' Kate kept her eyes closed.

'You're not afraid any more to fly? Are you thinking of your little stone cottage?'

Kate smiled and nodded. 'It's on a hill next to a beautiful old vineyard. But that's not really what I'm thinking about.'

'Oh? What are you thinking about?'

There was an imperceptible pause.

'You.' Kate opened her eyes and turned towards Luc. They looked at each other for a long moment, their faces unreadable, and then Luc took her hand.

'And I am thinking that you should not be flying anywhere. I am thinking, I want you . . .' He left the sentence unfinished.

Kate smiled. 'You want me . . .'

'That's all. I want you.' He leaned forward slowly and kissed her.

Then he reached down and undid her seatbelt, took her hand and led her to the heavy door of the plane, and demanded that they be let off.

It took all of the will-power and strength that they had to wait until they were in the tiny abandoned stone cottage, overlooking their vineyard, before they finally made love.